FROZEN SUMMER

OKTAY EGE KOZAK

120
pages

HOW TO READ A SCREENPLAY

A screenplay is written to show, not tell. Screenplays convey how a film will play out. The story unfolds through the dialogue and actions of the characters. As such, words are used economically. There is less description than you would find in a novel, as those details are typically handled during the production process. There is very little exposition; the screenplay doesn't provide any information that an audience watching the film wouldn't receive.

Therefore, as you read, visualize a film in your mind and "see" it as if you were watching a film.

If you're not familiar with the screenplay format, here are some things to know:

SCENE HEADINGS

Scene headings describe where the action takes place, the time of day, and sometimes additional details, such as if the action takes place in a flashback or as part of a montage.

For example:

```
INT. SAMMY'S HOUSE - DAY
```

"INT" indicates the action is indoors. "SAMMY'S HOUSE" tells us the action is in a woman's house. "DAY" tells us that it is daytime.

```
EXT. PARK - NIGHT
```

"EXT" indicates the action is outdoors. "PARK" tells us we are in a park. "NIGHT" tells us that it is the evening.

Other time descriptions may be used, such as "SAME" to indicate action taking place simultaneously or "LATER" to indicate action taking place moments later, after a brief jump in time.

CAPITALIZED WORDS

Throughout a screenplay, you may come across CAPITALIZED WORDS. These generally indicate the introduction of a new character, that the camera should pay attention to a particular item/sound/person/location, or that we are moving into a specific place within the location.

For example:

```
John turns.  He sees SALLY, the most beautiful girl he has ever
laid eyes on.  In her hands, she holds AN ADORABLE PUPPY.
```

DIALOGUE

Dialogue is written by centering a character's name with their spoken words appearing beneath their name. For example:

```
                    JOHN
          You found Charlie!
```

PARANTHETICALS

Between the character's name and dialogue, you may see text in parenthesis. This indicates some specific direction about how the dialogue is to be read or some specific action that takes place during the delivery of the dialogue.

```
                    JOHN
              (eyes watering)
          You found Charlie!
```

OTHER TERMS

Here are some other terms you may come across when reading a screenplay:

(O.S.) or (O.C.) – Off-screen or off-camera indicates that we do not see a character when dialogue is heard

(V.O.) – Indicates voiceover. This is dialogue we hear, but the speaker is not physically present in the same location as the action

(CONT'D) – Indicates that the same character is continuing to deliver a line of dialogue after an action, scene change, or page break

(MORE) – Indicates that the dialogue from the character continues on the next page

POV – Indicates that we see the action through a defined point of view

SUPERIMPOSE – Indicates that we see text on screen, often to define a time or location

MONTAGE – Indicates rapid cutting of different scenes in a sequence, such as any training sequence in a Rocky movie

(beat) – Indicates that a character takes a brief pause before continuing dialogue

FROZEN SUMMER

Gold Prize, 2013 Beverly Hills Screenplay Contest
Honorable Mention, 2014 Screenplay Festival
3rd Place, 2015 Reddit Screenwriting Contest
Quarter Finalist, 2012 Slamdance Film Festival

CREDITS SEQUENCE

Hundreds of complex scientific equations fly before our eyes.
Numbers crash and dissolve, some superimpose--

> MAX (35) (V.O.)
> Memories are strange. We always
> want to remember our most
> incredible achievements but end up
> remembering the smallest, most
> unimportant pieces of our past.

INT. BENJAMIN FRANKLIN HIGH SCHOOL / CAFETERIA — DAY

A STUDENT'S POV, walking through the cafeteria, which is--

Crawling with YOUNG STUDENTS, all going through their
feverish adolescent phase.

They run around and laugh (MOS).

The numbers and equations float around the students, showing
a mathematical visualization of their actions.

A STUDENT playfully kicks another STUDENT. The velocity and
the angle of the kick are superimposed on the POV as if
sketched on a notebook.

> MAX (35) (V.O.)
> It's strange when you think about
> how all those memories you hold
> close to your heart are tiny little
> fragments of your brain cells,
> operating on electricity. Yet as we
> grow older, they become our most
> prized possessions.

A couple of GIRLS walk by grinning at each other. Numbers
appear around their smiling mouths, showing the angles of
their smiles.

A group of BOYS stroll behind them, leering at the girls.

One BOY playfully throws gum to a GIRL's hair. The schematics
and numbers show the scientific details of the gum hitting
her hair and getting stuck. The girl curses the guy. (MOS)

> MAX (35) (V.O.
> I don't remember every event that
> surrounds my life. But I do
> remember that summer. And I do
> remember Doug, Amanda… and Sandy.
> (MORE)

                    MAX (35) (V.O. (CONT'D)
          And although I always believed in
          rationality, there is no rational
          way to tell this story. Sometimes I
          don't even believe it myself.

A big group of STUDENTS throw food at each other. As the POV
Student makes his way through them, the numbers collide and
explode along with the food.

                    MAX (35) (V.O.)(CONT'D)
          That doesn't mean it didn't happen.

The POV student sits at an empty table, away from other
students. He opens TWO DIRTY NOTEBOOKS, full of complex math
problems. He is--

MAX SCHRODINGER, 13, a skinny kid, average looks, dressed
like a fifty-year-old accountant.

As we cut away from the POV, the floating numbers disappear.

Max scribbles more complex math problems on the notebooks.

Three boys, LARRY, GREG and VINCE are playfully arguing at a
nearby table. Greg notices Max.

                    GREG
          Hey Vince. Vince!

                    VINCE
          What?

                    GREG
          Nerd alert. Six o'clock.

Vince grins with pleasure.

All three parade toward Max's table. They surround him.

                    GREG (CONT'D)
          Hey Max, What's up?

Max doesn't even lift his head.

                    MAX
          Hi Vince.

Vince pulls up a chair and sits uncomfortably close to Max.

                    VINCE
          You know we're on break?

                    MAX
          Yes.

                    GREG
          You know what break means?

                    MAX
          Yes.

                    VINCE
          I don't think he does. You see
          Max, break means you don't work.

                    MAX
          So?

                    GREG
          It looks like you keep working.
          And that makes us look bad.

Greg rips off a couple of pages from Max's notebook.

Max is furious but doesn't act on it.

Greg taps hard on Max's head.

                    GREG (CONT'D)
          Check you later.

                    LARRY
          Bye, loser.

Greg, Larry and Vince leave, laughing at Max.

Max buries his head back to his work.

He gazes around the room. Some KIDS give him the stink eye.

He quickly picks up his stuff and leaves.

CAFETERIA EXIT

Greg, Larry and Vince strut out of the cafeteria.

                    VINCE
          What a freak man!

INT. BENJAMIN FRANKLIN HIGH SCHOOL / PRINCIPAL'S OFFICE — DAY

PRINCIPAL McKENNA, 46, stands behind his desk, flips through
a student's file.

                    MCKENNA
          What a genius!

The name on the file reads "Max Schrodinger".

4.

He closes the file and presses the intercom.

> MCKENNA (CONT'D)
> Kate, can you tell Ms. Schrodinger
> she can come in?

> KATE(O.S.)
> Yes Mr. McKenna

McKenna sits on his office chair.

The door opens. EVELYN, 40, enters.

She looks like a regular mom, beaten down by the facts of life but still holding onto the gleam in her eye.

She wears strict business clothes with a name tag.

> EVELYN
> Principal McKenna?

> MCKENNA
> Hello Ms. Schrodinger. Please, sit.

> EVELYN
> Evelyn, please.

> MCKENNA
> Of course, Evelyn.

Evelyn sits.

> EVELYN
> Sorry for being so late. One of my
> sessions went on too long.

> MCKENNA
> It's okay. What do you do?

> EVELYN
> I'm an occupational social analyst.
> I give seminars to corporations
> about communication ethics.

Evelyn notices her name tag. She takes it off, folds it and puts it in her pocket.

> EVELYN (CONT'D)
> So, what's this about?

> MCKENNA
> It's your son.

Evelyn's not surprised--

                    EVELYN
          Chet. What did he do now?

                    MCKENNA
          No. This is about Max.

Now she's surprised.

                    EVELYN
          Max? What happened, did he upset
          another math teacher?

                    MCKENNA
          Yes, but that's not why I called
          you here.

McKenna peeks at Max's file.

                    MCKENNA (CONT'D)
          I noticed on your file that the
          field for the second parent is
          empty. Is Max still in touch with
          his father?

Evelyn is uncomfortable by the question. There is still some
pain there.

                    EVELYN
          His father and I are... Separated.

                    MCKENNA
          I'm sorry, I didn't mean to pry.
          What I need to discuss with you, I
          was just wondering if he would be
          interested in...

                    EVELYN
          He's not. He's been away, for a
          while. I make decisions for my son.

McKenna picks up on Evelyn's discomfort--

                    MCKENNA
          Fair enough. The reason I called
          you here is, I have great news.

Evelyn is intrigued.

                    MCKENNA (CONT'D)
          Max got into O.I.T..

Evelyn looks mildly excited yet disappointed. McKenna is
surprised by Evelyn's reaction.

                    EVELYN
          O.I.T. huh?

                    MCKENNA
          Yes, The Oregon Institute of
          Technology. It's a university for
          highly gifted kids.

                    EVELYN
          I know what it is.

                    D'SOUZA
          Honestly, I thought you'd be more
          thrilled. Being able to go to
          O.I.T. at Max's age, it happens
          once, almost every decade. Your son
          will become a great scientist one
          day. Perhaps one of the greatest.

Evelyn sighs.

                    EVELYN
          That's what I'm afraid of.

McKenna is baffled by Evelyn's response.

                    MCKENNA
          Ms. Schrodinger... Evelyn, are you
          aware of the extent of your son's
          scientific and mathematical genius?

McKenna picks up Max's file.

He gets up, looks at the file while walking around.

                    MCKENNA (CONT'D)
          Last week, the head of our math
          department wrote an extremely
          complicated problem on the board
          for anyone who wished to get an A.
          Max not only solved the problem in
          less than a minute, he wrote
          another one for the department head
          to solve.

                    EVELYN
          I know Max is very talented when it
          comes to math. But what's so
          incredibly special about that?

McKenna stops and turns to Evelyn.

                    MCKENNA
          He couldn't solve it.

Evelyn doesn't look surprised. McKenna continues walking.

                    MCKENNA (CONT'D)
          Max gives lectures to teachers
          during breaks, he builds complex
          machines in minutes. Other kids use
          his brain as a human calculator.

McKenna sits back down.

                    MCKENNA (CONT'D)
          Evelyn, we here at Benjamin
          Franklin High School pride
          ourselves in being the best
          possible educational institution
          for our young ones. But after the
          end of this year, we realized that
          Max has surpassed the academic
          level of pretty much everyone in
          this establishment. I don't think
          it would be fair to him if he
          stayed here. Do you?

Evelyn looks uncomfortable, conflicted.

McKenna pulls out some forms and drops them on the desk.

                    MCKENNA (CONT'D)
          We arranged everything as far as
          his application goes. All you have
          to do is sign these forms.

Evelyn picks up the forms and looks at them for a while. She
looks uncomfortable.

                    MCKENNA (CONT'D)
          What's wrong?

                    EVELYN
          May I think about this?

                    MCKENNA
          Take your time. The paperwork has
          to be sent in by next month or Max
          will miss an entire year.

Evelyn nods. She looks at the forms, worried.

EXT. SCHRODINGER APARTMENT — NIGHT

An apartment BUILDING in the middle-class part of a
metropolitan city.

INT. SCHRODINGER APARTMENT / ENTRANCE — NIGHT

Max enters and puts down his backpack.

> MAX
>
> Mom?

Nobody answers.

MAX'S ROOM

Filled with papers with math equations scribbled on them. It is chaotic and messy.

Max enters and turns on the stereo. "House of the Rising Sun" by Animals plays.

He turns to H.G., a Black European Hamster trying to operate the wheel in his small cage. Max wiggles his finger.

> MAX
>
> Hi H.G.

Max pulls out a Blueberry Pop Tart out of a Costco-sized box and starts eating it cold.

He sits down and thinks. He stares at the wall.

MAX'S POV shows numbers and complex equations pop up and fly around on the wall. They multiply in a chaotic way.

Max jumps to his notebook. He writes very fast, as if pouring out his head.

A bright light shines off of his head. Numbers pour out and begin to fill the room.

All of a sudden, Max hears--

A loud car engine from a distance. The numbers dissolve into thin air.

EXT. STREET

A cool car drives through the street in fast speed.

Laughing sounds echo from inside the car.

It stops in front of Max's apartment.

INT. BLAKE'S CAR (STOPPED)

BLAKE, CARRIE, AMY and CHET, all 18, pretty, popular.

Carrie sits next to Blake. Amy's next to Chet.

Carrie laughs--

                    CARRIE
          I can't believe you pulled it off!

                    BLAKE
          You bet your ass I did.

                    CHET
          Thanks for the ride.

                    BLAKE
          Alright man, I'll see you later.

                    AMY
          Bye baby.

Chet kisses Amy.

                    CHET
          Later.

                    BLAKE
          You're coming tonight, right?

                    CHET
          I don't know man. Mom said there's
          something going on with Max. I
          might have to stay in.

                    AMY
          What's up with your brother?

                    BLAKE
          What happened? Did his head finally
          blow up?

Everybody laughs.

MAX'S ROOM

Max slides open the curtains and looks at--

Blake's car. The laughing noises arise from the street.

BLAKE'S CAR (STOPPED)

Carrie jokingly hits Blake.

                    CARRIE
          You dick!

                         BLAKE
               What?! Chet's the one who always
               calls his brother a freak.

                         CHET
               That's right.

                         BLAKE
               See?

Chet gets out.

EXT. STREET

Chet walks to his building. Blake leans out of the car.

                         BLAKE
               Say hi to your retarded brother!

                         CHET
               I will, man! Later!

Blake's car leaves in the background.

INT. MAX'S ROOM

Max looks hurt. He closes the curtains, leaving himself in
the dark.

INT. SCHRODINGER APARTMENT / LIVING ROOM — NIGHT

Evelyn, Max and Chet sit around the dinner table, eating
delivery food.

                         CHET
               So mom, what's the big news?

Max lifts his head from his food in anticipation.

                         EVELYN
               I'll tell you after dinner.

                         CHET
               Just get it over with, will you? I
               wanna hang out with the guys later.

                         EVELYN
               You can't go out tonight. You got
               school this week.

                         CHET
               You know nobody studies the last
               week of school. Just spill it.

                    EVELYN
          Max got into O.I.T.

Max drops his fork in pure excitement.

                    MAX
          Really?

                    EVELYN
          That's the first time I've seen you
          smile all week.

                    CHET
          What's O.I.T.?

                    EVELYN
          It's a university for gifted kids.

                    CHET
          You mean nerds?

                    EVELYN
          Chet!

                    CHET
          Isn't he too young for college?

                    EVELYN
          Since he's quite the genius, your
          brother's taking the fast track.

                    MAX
          When do I start?

                    EVELYN
          I don't know sweetie.

Max looks stunned.

                    MAX
          What do you mean you don't know?

                    EVELYN
          It means I'm not sure going to
          O.I.T. would be best for you.

                    MAX
          What are you talking about? Of
          course it is.

Evelyn pets Max on the shoulder.

12.

                    EVELYN
          Honey, I know you have a special
          gift that no one your age has. But
          each year, I watch you become more
          reclusive than the last.

Max pulls himself away from Evelyn.

                    MAX
          So what?

                    EVELYN
          So what!? You bury yourself in your
          work. You don't have any friends.
          You don't even say more than five
          words to me every week. You just--

Evelyn stops herself. She takes a deep, cleansing breath.

                    EVELYN (CONT'D)
          Look at me. It's like I'm talking
          about your father. The bottom line
          is, I'm not sure if O.I.T. is a
          good idea.

                    CHET
          How do you know that? Maybe he'll
          finally have some friends. You
          know, if he's around other...

                    EVELYN
          I deal with O.I.T. grads all the
          time. They're zombies with laptops.
          You wouldn't know they're alive
          unless you poked them with a stick.

Evelyn turns to Max.

                    EVELYN (CONT'D)
          I don't want that to be you.

Max tries to calm himself down.

                    MAX
          Listen mom. I'm working on things
          people like you can't even begin to
          imagine. In years, when I become
          the most successful scientist that
          ever lived, no one will care how
          many people were at my fifteenth
          birthday party.

                    EVELYN
          I'm sorry honey.

Max stands up in anger.

                    MAX
          First dad betrayed me, now you!!

He throws a plate at the wall.

                    MAX (CONT'D)
          I hate you!!

Max storms back to his room and slams the door.

Evelyn and Chet look at each other in silence.

Evelyn looks full of thought.

                    EVELYN
          Clean up the table.

INT. MAX'S ROOM - NIGHT

Intensely focused, Max works on--

A rough schematic of an octagon-shaped machine.

There's a knock on the door.

                    EVELYN (O.S.)
          Can I come in?

Max hides the schematic in a drawer.

                    MAX
          Whatever.

Evelyn enters. She stays near the doorway.

                    EVELYN
          Do you know what your father wanted
          to name you?

                    MAX
          I don't care.

                    EVELYN
          Alexander. He wanted to see his son
          outsmarting everyone in the room
          with that name. It's a strong name,
          he used to say, 'A perfect name for
          a genius'. But I vehemently
          disagreed. I had already lost the
          name battle with Chet.

Max snickers--

                    MAX
          Remember when he was in fifth
          grade, he beat me up because I told
          his friends that Chet is short for
          Chester? They called him Chester
          Cheetah for two years.

Evelyn tries to control her laugh but fails.

                    EVELYN
          Anyway, I insisted on naming you
          Max. Somehow, we both knew how
          smart you would become. I guess I
          figured if your name was Max, you
          wouldn't be as cold and distant.

Max smiles. He turns around.

                    MAX
          Mom, do you want me to be happy?

                    EVELYN
          Of course I do.

                    MAX
          Then let me go.

Max shows Evelyn his equations.

                    MAX (CONT'D)
          This is my life, it's what I want
          to do with the rest of it. I'm
          happy doing it. Shouldn't that mean
          something to you?

Evelyn looks deep in thought.

EVELYN'S ROOM

Evelyn lies in her bed, reading a magazine.

She picks up the O.I.T. forms from her nightstand. She puts
them on top of the magazine. She picks up a pen.

Right when she is about to sign, she notices--

An ad that reads, 'Come to Lake Vonnegut: Live The Summer of
Your Dreams!!'

The ad shows pictures of a crystal clear lake, beautiful
misty mountain hills and a tranquil forest.

Evelyn looks intrigued--

EXT. HIGHWAY TO LAKE — DAY

The road is surrounded by the serenity of the trees.

The Schrodinger family car runs alone within nature.

INT. SCHRODINGER FAMILY CAR (MOVING)

Evelyn drives while Chet sits beside her. Max is in the back
seat. Next to him, H.G. sleeps in his cage.

Chet plays a game on his PS Vita.

Max blows on the car window to create a mist. He uses his
finger to write a quick equation.

Finished with his equation, he becomes bored and sits in the
middle, huffing and puffing.

>   EVELYN
>   Remember what we agreed on. No
>   bitching until we're there.

>   MAX
>   We are there. Don't you see the
>   mountains, the trees, the lack of
>   civilization?

>   EVELYN
>   Can't you at least hold off till we
>   get to the Lake? Maybe once we're
>   there, you'll see this wasn't such
>   a bad idea.

>   MAX
>   Of course it was a bad idea. I'd
>   have been fine back home.

Chet pauses the game.

>   CHET
>   Me too mom. I understand that you
>   wanted to spend more time with Max
>   so the little freak would start
>   saying things other than "I'm
>   Bored" and "Leave me alone". But I
>   have no idea why you had to drag me
>   into this?

>   EVELYN
>   Don't test me Chet.

Chet turns his attention back to the game while Max leans on
his seat. They both look bored.

                         EVELYN (CONT'D)
               Come on guys! This is the first
               time we're doing anything together
               as a family in years. You can
               either keep moaning about something
               you can't change, or you can sit
               back and enjoy it.

Evelyn turns on the radio. A cheesy romantic song from the
80s plays. Evelyn hums along to the song. Chet covers his
ears with all his might.

EXT. HIGHWAY

The car enters a parking lot next to a strip of shops.

The car parks at the space closest to the grocery shop.

INT. SCHRODINGER FAMILY CAR (STOPPED)

Evelyn turns the ignition off.

                         EVELYN
               Alright boys. This is our final
               stop. Let's grab everything we can.

Evelyn and Chet step out of the car.

Max picks up H.G.'s cage and gets out.

EXT. STORE PARKING LOT

Evelyn walks into the store. Chet looks at H.G., disgusted.

                         CHET
               Do you really have to take that
               thing everywhere?

                         MAX
               Yes.

                         CHET
               Just stay away from me.

                         EVELYN
               Chet, come on.

Chet follows Evelyn.

STORE ENTRANCE

Evelyn, Chet and Max are about to enter.

The STORE OWNER yells from inside. He points at H.G.--

                    STORE OWNER
          I'm sorry ma'am, I can't let you in
          with that animal.

Evelyn turns to Max.

                    EVELYN
          Can you leave H.G. in the car?

                    MAX
          He needs some air.

                    EVELYN
          I know. Why don't you stay by the
          car, as my strong security guard?

Evelyn rubs Max's hair. Max rolls his eyes.

                    MAX
          Whatever.

                    EVELYN
          We'll be back in a minute.

Evelyn and Chet enter the store.

Max sits on the pavement, bored.

MAX'S POV shows FAMILIES enter and exit the stores.

Numbers appear around the families. Every move they make is
shown with scientific equations.

Suddenly, Max notices--

An OVERWEIGHT, BALDING MAN, 50s, leans on his car, completely
still. The numbers don't appear around him, as if he's immune
to them.

He eats ice cream, petting an OLD LARGE DOG who sits by his
side.

Even though he's wearing sunglasses, it looks like he's
staring at Max. The Dog is definitely looking at him.

Max nervously smiles and waves. The Middle-Aged Man smiles
and waves back.

The Man looks like he remembered something important. He
turns his head to the store entrance.

Curious to see what the Middle-Aged Man is looking at, Max
turns as well.

MAX'S POV: He notices a 13-YEAR-OLD GIRL walking in the store
with her FAMILY. All of the numbers that were floating around
suddenly crash and explode.

Max is enticed by the girl. Nerdy but elegant, she looks like
she doesn't belong in her age group.

She stops by the magazine stand and picks up a copy of The
Oregonian. She gazes through it.

> THE GIRL'S MOTHER (O.S.)
> Come on honey, let's go!

The girl enters the store. Max tracks her with his eyes until
she disappears from his sight.

Max turns back to look at the Middle-Aged Man with the dog.
He's gone.

Evelyn and Chet exit with full grocery bags.

Chet realizes the confusion on Max's face.

> CHET
> What happened to you?

Max gets a grip.

> MAX
> Nothing.

He gets up and follows Evelyn and Chet.

> CHET
> Are we leaving now?

> EVELYN
> No. We got one more thing.

EXT. STORE PARKING LOT — DAY (MOMENTS LATER)

Chet adjusts a camera placed on the hood of the car.

> CHET
> This is really dumb.

Evelyn and Max stand next to the car with the beautiful
mountain view in the background.

> EVELYN
> Stop complaining. I want a family
> photo before we get there. Do you
> see the mountain behind us?

                    CHET
              (*without looking*)
          Yeah, sure.

Chet presses a button and stands next to Evelyn.

                    EVELYN
          Alright everybody, smile!

No one smiles.

                    EVELYN (CONT'D)
          Okay, imagine we're going back to
          the city.

Max and Chet smile from ear to ear.

Evelyn scoffs. FLASH. FREEZE on the picture.

EXT. LAKE VONNEGUT / ENTRANCE — DAY

The Schrodinger family car drives through the entrance gate.

BEGIN MONTAGE - LAKE VONNEGUT

--The family car drives through the lake.

--Majestic views of the mysterious mountain terrain with the beautiful lake side visible in the background.

--People, kids, families swim and kayak in the calm waters of the river.

--A common area shack where kids hang out outside. They eat snacks and ice cream.

--People play in the outdoor basketball courts.

--The family car approaches the long line of houses, one glued next to the other.

--END MONTAGE--

EXT. SCHRODINGER FAMILY HOUSE - DAY

The family car stops in front of a duplex house that looks like it was made specifically for nostalgic summer vacations.

It's perched at the edge of the cliff, has a small porch at the entrance so that residents can enjoy the beautiful view of the mountain.

Evelyn gets out of the car.

                              EVELYN
                    Look at that! Isn't it amazing?

Chet gets out.

                              CHET
                    I guess.

                              EVELYN
                    Boys, say "Hi" to our new home.

                              CHET
                    Do you have to call it that?

Evelyn picks up boxes from the trunk. Chet does the same.

                              EVELYN
                    Max, honey, can you grab some of
                    the bags from the back?

Max gets out of the car and opens the back door.

He picks up a couple of bags and turns around. He stops to
look at--

The large dog from the store. He stands on the porch of the
house next to his. The dog stares directly at Max.

Max looks intrigued.

The dog turns to the door of his house. He barks--

The Middle-Aged Man from the store walks out of the shack.

He pets the dog while looking out at the view. He notices
Max. He smiles and waves at him.

Max gives a shy half-smile and nods back.

The Man turns to look at Evelyn as she carries grocery bags
inside. They lock eyes.

The Man looks oddly emotional when he sees Evelyn. Evelyn
looks uncomfortable, but feels an odd connection.

The Man gets a grip. He nods and smiles. Evelyn half-smiles
back. As Chet walks by with a box--

                              CHET
                    What's up with that dude?

                              EVELYN
                    I don't know.

The Man walks back inside. The dog follows him.

Evelyn shakes off the uncomfortable feeling. She checks the
grocery bag.

                    EVELYN (CONT'D)
          Max.

Max, also entranced by the Man next door, turns to Evelyn.

                    MAX
          Yes?

                    EVELYN
          We forgot to buy paper towels. Can
          you walk to the store down the
          street and get some for me?

Evelyn gives a ten dollar bill to Max.

Max reluctantly takes it.

                    EVELYN (CONT'D)
          Thanks sweetie.

Evelyn kisses Max on the forehead and walks back. Max takes
one last look at the house next door and leaves.

EXT. LAKE VONNEGUT / STREET — DAY

Max walks on the side of the road with a bag filled with
paper towels in one hand and H.G. in the other.

A YOUNG BOY, 13, riding a scooter, approaches from a
distance. He is skinny, wears outrageous colors that make him
look desperate for attention.

He wears a hat that's too large for his head.

He slows down when he reaches Max and strolls beside him.

Max looks annoyed by his presence.

                    DOUG
          Hi. Welcome to Lake Vonnegut!

The kid offers his hand. Max doesn't respond.

                    DOUG (CONT'D)
          What's your name?

                    MAX
          Max.

22.

                         DOUG
              I'm Doug. Where are you from?

Max doesn't answer.

                         DOUG (CONT'D)
              You don't wanna talk, huh? I
              understand. Some people, they don't
              like talking. I love it. Talking
              with friends, hangin' out.

Max casually switches to the other side of the road. Doug
follows him.

                         DOUG (CONT'D)
              I don't have a lot of friends right
              now but someday I plan on
              overcoming that obstacle. It must
              have been hard to leave all your
              friends back home, wherever you're
              from, and come all the way here?
              Cute hamster, is it yours?

                         MAX
              Yes.

                         DOUG
              What's his name?

                         MAX
              H.G.

                         DOUG
              Hi H.G.! I really like hamsters. I
              like all animals...

Max interrupts Doug.

                         MAX
              I have to go home, okay? So please,
              leave me alone.

Max walks while Doug remains immobile.

                         DOUG
              Funny, that's what everyone says.

Doug follows Max.

                         DOUG (CONT'D)
              Isn't that weird?

                         MAX
              Not really.

There is an awkward silence.

>   DOUG
>   So, do you like scooters?

>   MAX
>   Not really.

>   DOUG
>   I love scooters. I can do all kinds
>   of tricks with mine. Here, let me
>   show you.

Doug blasts off with his scooter.

He turns a curve in front of Max and pulls up the front wheel
while turning it around.

The back wheel of the scooter hits a big stone, throwing Doug
and the scooter in the air!

Doug lands on the ground. The scooter crashes next to him.
Max reluctantly walks up to Doug to see if he's okay.

Doug jumps up and checks himself.

>   DOUG (CONT'D)
>   I'm alive. Whoo hoo!

He looks at the scooter.

>   DOUG (CONT'D)
>   Oh no!

Smoke comes out of the scooter.

Doug picks up the scooter and turns it on. It doesn't run.

Max stands next to Doug.

>   DOUG (CONT'D)
>   Mom's gonna kill me! Do you know
>   anything about fixing this stuff?

Max sighs.

>   MAX
>   If I fix your scooter, do you
>   promise to leave me alone?

>   DOUG
>   I swear.

Max approaches the scooter. He opens up the hatch.

MAX'S POV shows the wires inside the scooter. Like the POV of
The Terminator, Max locates the problems within the wiring.

Max re-assembles the wires in a manner of seconds.

He gives the scooter to Doug.

Doug turns it on. It's working.

> DOUG (CONT'D)
> Wow! You're a genius.

Max looks slightly full of himself.

> DOUG (CONT'D)
> I guess I'll see you later… Or not,
> you know…

Max almost cracks out a smile.

> MAX
> Bye.

Max walks off.

Doug looks behind him, disappointed--

> DOUG
> Bye.

Doug leaves the other way on his scooter.

EXT. SCHRODINGER HOME — NIGHT

Only one room has the lights on.

INT. MAX'S ROOM

Max writes on his notebook, with the desk light on. H.G.
sleeps in his cage.

The numbers fly around the room. They are more chaotic than
before, they crash into each other and dissolve. Suddenly,
they all explode and disappear.

Exhausted and frustrated, Max leans back on his chair, in
deep thought.

All of a sudden, he notices something outside. He leans to
the window.

The Balding Man stands in front of the house with his dog,
staring at Max's room. Max is creeped out.

The Man leaves. Max sits back on his chair, pondering.

EXT. SCHRODINGER HOUSE — DAY

The house shines under the bright sunlight.

INT. UPSTAIRS CORRIDOR

Evelyn comes out of the bathroom with a basket full of laundry. She puts it down and catches her breath.

She looks at Max's door. It has a "Do Not Enter" sign.

MAX'S ROOM

Max works on the schematic of the octagon-shaped machine.

There's a knock on the door. Max hides the schematic.

> EVELYN
> What are you doing?

> MAX
> Just, working. What do you want?

> EVELYN
> I'm going to the lake. Do you want
> to come?

> MAX
> I can't.

> EVELYN
> Sure you can. It's been two days
> and all you've done so far is,
> working. I want you downstairs in
> five minutes.

> MAX
> But mom!

> EVELYN
> Five minutes!

Evelyn exits. Max scoffs.

EXT. LAKE — DAY

YOUNG PEOPLE, FAMILIES swimming, kayaking.

Evelyn, Chet and Max sit under a large tree. H.G. sits next to Max in his cage.

Max solves a math problem on the sand, using a stick.

Evelyn looks around the lake.

                    EVELYN
          Isn't this nice?

                    CHET
          Yeah, it's awesome. Can I go hang
          with my friends now?

                    EVELYN
          No. As your mother, I'm requesting
          at least an hour of family time
          with you.

                    CHET
          A day!?

Evelyn nods.

Chet scoffs. A shadow covers the family's sun.

                    PLUMP WOMAN (O.S.)
          Hi there.

The shadow belongs to a HEAVY-SET WOMAN, 40s, with an
outrageously friendly smile.

Doug stands next to the plump woman.

                    PLUMP WOMAN (CONT'D)
          You must be Evelyn, cabin 237?

Evelyn looks clueless.

                    PLUMP WOMAN (CONT'D)
          I'm Rose, we talked on the phone?

                    EVELYN
          Oh yes. You're the resident
          manager. Nice to meet you.

Evelyn shakes Rose's hand.

                    EVELYN (CONT'D)
          You too. Who's this little guy?

Rose scratches Doug's hair. Doug doesn't like it.

                    ROSE
          This is my son, Dougie. Apparently
          him and your son met already.

Evelyn turns to Max.

                    EVELYN
          Max! I didn't know you already
          found a friend. That's great!

Max looks annoyed.

                    ROSE
          Care for a little walk?

                    EVELYN
          Of course not. I will be right back
          Max. Stay here with your friend.

                    MAX
          He's not my... Okay.

Rose and Evelyn walk toward the forest.

                    ROSE
          Play safe Dougie!

Doug reluctantly waves at Rose and turns to Max.

                    DOUG
          I hate it when she calls me that.

Doug sits next to Max. Chet stands up.

                    CHET
          Wow! You look like you were made
          for each other.

                    BONNIE (O.S.)
          Hey Chet!

Chet turns around. Two hot eighteen-year-old girls, BONNIE
and CRIS, wave at Chet while passing by on their kayak.

                    CHET
          I'll be right there!
               (to himself)
          Nice.

Chet runs off.

Doug and Max sit quietly for a while. Max focuses on his
equation on the sand.

                    DOUG
          I'm sorry about breaking your
          'leave me alone' rule. I had every
          intention of upholding it but it
          seems like our parents somehow got
          in the way.

28.

                    MAX
          Uh-huh.

                    DOUG
          So, what are you writing?

                    MAX
          You wouldn't understand.

                    DOUG
          You're right, I don't. Why don't
          you use a computer for all that?

                    MAX
          I don't know.

                    DOUG
          I guess when you're smarter than a
          computer you don't really need one,
          huh? I'm a total idiot when it
          comes to math stuff. I'm pretty
          good with computers though, isn't
          that strange?

Doug looks around, bored. He notices the small snack shack
next to the riverside.

                    DOUG (CONT'D)
          Do you want some ice cream?

                    MAX
          Sure, whatever.

Doug looks for money in his backpack. Max notices--

The nerdy girl from the grocery store waiting in line by
herself to buy some snacks.

Doug grabs the money and walks toward the shack.

                    MAX (CONT'D)
          Doug, wait!

Doug stops and turns around--

                    DOUG
          What?

                    MAX
          I'll get it.

                    DOUG
          Are you sure? I'm like almost
          halfway there.

                    MAX
          It's cool, I got it.

Doug sits back down. Max walks to the vendor. He can not take
his eyes off the girl.

He stands next to the girl, trying to divert his eyes.

The CLERK gives ice cream to the girl.

                    CLERK
          Here you go little lady.

                    NERDY GIRL
          Thank you.

She reaches in her beach purse and pulls out some money. Some
change falls on the sand.

Max attempts to pick up the change but hesitates. Doug
watches from a distance.

The girl looks at Max while Max still thinks. Awkward.

Max picks up the change. He gives the money to the girl. They
have slight hand contact.

                    NERDY GIRL (CONT'D)
          Thanks.

Max smiles and slightly nods.

The girl pays the clerk and leaves, giving a last nervous
recognition look at Max.

Max is fixated on the girl. Doug watches Max, grinning.

Max picks up the ice cream and walks back to Doug.

                    DOUG
          Now I see why you wanted to buy.

Max sits down.

                    MAX
          What do you mean?

                    DOUG
          You love that girl.

                    MAX
          No I don't.

Doug eats his ice cream while Max lets it melt.

                    DOUG
          Yeah you do. I saw it. You're
          totally in love with her.

                    MAX
          No I'm not!

                    DOUG
          Sure, whatever.

Doug smiles behind Max. Max is fixated on--

The girl as she disappears into the forest.

EXT. FOREST — DAY

A sign on a tree advertising a party on August 20 at the main
gathering site.

Max has H.G. in one hand and his notebook in the other.
Evelyn walks next to him.

In the distance, he notices a MAN, 40s. He talks to a WOMAN
with his back turned (MOS).

                    MAX
          Mom?

                    EVELYN
          Yes?

                    MAX
          Is it okay if I take a walk? You
          know, let H.G. get some air?

                    EVELYN
          Of course it's alright. Have fun.
          Be home by dinner time.

Evelyn leaves. Max walks towards the man.

                    MAX
          Dad?

The man disappears behind the trees. Max runs.

                    MAX (CONT'D)
          Dad!

Max stops, disappointed and lost. He sits on a trunk.

A dog's nose nudges against his hand. Max looks at the dog;
it's the dog from next door.

                    SANDY (O.S.)
          Hi there.

Max looks up. The Balding Man from next door stands in front
of him, looking very out of place.

                    MAX
          Hello.

                    SANDY
          Didn't you just move in next door?

                    MAX
          Yes.

                    SANDY
          I'm Sandy Planck.

                    MAX
          Hi Mr. Planck, I'm Max.

                    SANDY
          You can call me Sandy.

                    MAX
          I'd prefer Mr. Planck.

                    SANDY
          I wouldn't.

                    MAX
          Why not?

                    SANDY
          When you grow up, you'll be calling
          a lot of people by their last name.
          I'd rather be the exception. Do you
          mind if I sit?

                    MAX
          No, go ahead.

Sandy sits next to Max.

                    SANDY
          Cute hamster. Is it yours?

                    MAX
          Yes. This is H.G.

                    SANDY
          Clever name.

The dog sneaks his head under Max's hand. Max pets him.

32.

                    MAX
          And he is?

                    SANDY
          Albert.

                    MAX
          Clever name.

Sandy smiles.

                    SANDY
          So, do you go to school Max?

                    MAX
          I used to go to a High School. But
          next year, I'm going to O.I.T..

                    SANDY
          Wow, O.I.T. huh? You must be a
          smart kid.

                    MAX
          I hope so. Are you a scientist?

Sandy smiles.

                    SANDY
          What gave it away? My complete
          disregard to fashion or my amazing
          social skills?

Max laughs.

                    SANDY (CONT'D)
          Yes, I am one of those unfortunate
          souls. At least I used to be. But
          now I'm nothing but a crazy old man
          with a dog as old as time.

Sandy looks at Max's notebook.

                    MAX
          What do you have there?

                    SANDY
          Oh, this? Just some math.

                    MAX
          Do you mind?

Max looks at his notebook. He is unsure.

                    MAX (CONT'D)
          Sure, I guess.

Max gives the notebook to Sandy. Sandy gazes through it.

                    SANDY
          This is hard stuff. I'm impressed.

Sandy looks at the final page.

                    SANDY (CONT'D)
          Ouch. This one's a killer.

Sandy pulls out his PEN.

                    SANDY (CONT'D)
          May I?

                    MAX
          Go ahead.

Sandy writes on the notebook.

                    MAX (CONT'D)
          I've been working on that one for
          three weeks now. It's impossible.

Sandy gives the notebook back to Max.

Max looks at the page. He is shocked.

                    MAX (CONT'D)
          Wow! How did you do that?

                    SANDY
          That's nothing kid. It's having
          people around to share it with,
          that's the hardest part. I'll see
          you later.

Sandy taps on Max's shoulder and leaves. Albert follows him.

Max looks at Sandy as he leaves. He is impressed.

INT. SCHRODINGER HOUSE / MAX'S ROOM — DAY

Max sits alone in his room, stares at his notebook.

He picks up a pencil.

                    DOUG (O.S.)
          Max! Hey Max!

Max drops his pencil and sighs.

EXT. PORCH

Doug looks up at Max's window, holding a basketball. Max leans over the window.

> MAX
> What do you want?

> DOUG
> How's it goin' bro?

> MAX
> What do you want?

Doug holds up the ball.

> DOUG
> You wanna play ball?

> MAX
> No.

> DOUG
> Come on!

> MAX
> No! I got a lot of work to do.

> DOUG
> Pleeeease?

> MAX
> No.

Doug dances like a mentally challenged cheerleader.

> DOUG
> *(singing off-key)*
> Come on Max, let's shoot some
> hoops. It will be fun because I
> like basketball and you like
> basketball and basketball is fun!

> MAX
> Okay! I'll be right down. Just
> promise me you'll never do that
> ever again.

EXT. BASKETBALL COURT — DAY

Doug takes shots while Max sits on the corner, writing on his notebook. None of Doug's shots go in.

Doug runs and grabs the ball.

                    DOUG
          You wanna shoot?

                    MAX
          I never played before.

Doug takes a shot. Doesn't even come close.

                    DOUG
          You never played basketball!? It's
          a piece of cake. Just shoot the
          ball. If it goes into that round
          thing, you win.

                    MAX
          I figured that much.

Doug gives the ball to Max. Max reluctantly walks up to the
shooting line.

Max throws the ball. It doesn't even reach the hoop.

                    DOUG
          Wow, that was weak man.

                    MAX
          It's not like you were any better.

Doug picks up the ball and gives it back to Max.

                    DOUG
          Here, give it another shot.

Max prepares for the shot.

                    DOUG (CONT'D)
          So, that girl from the lake. Are
          you in love with her?

                    MAX
          I don't even know her.

                    DOUG
          I can help you with that.

                    MAX
          How?

Max takes a shot. It doesn't go in.

                    DOUG
          I'll look into my mom's files. I
          can also follow her around.

Doug runs after the ball.

> MAX
> Isn't that illegal, and a little
> bit creepy?

> DOUG
> Nooo.

Doug passes to Max. Max grins at Doug.

> CRAIG (O.S.)
> Hey asshole!

Max and Doug turn around. CRAIG and DEREK, 15, strong and
mean boys, approach them.

> CRAIG (CONT'D)
> This is our court. Get lost.

> DOUG
> Just play the other side.

> DEREK
> We wanna play on both sides.

> DOUG
> Why?

Craig grabs Doug.

> CRAIG
> Listen you weirdo, we told you to
> get lost!

Craig pushes Doug to the floor. Derek notices Max's notebook
on the ground.

> DEREK
> What the hell is this?

Derek picks up the notebook and sneers at it.

> MAX
> Don't touch that.

> DEREK
> What did you say kid?

> MAX
> I said don't touch that.

> DEREK
> What if I do?

Derek rips off a page from the notebook. Max runs at Derek and pushes him. Craig grabs Max.

> DEREK (CONT'D)
> You asked for this.

Derek lifts his fist to hit Max.

> SECURITY GUARD (O.S.)
> Hey, what's going on over there?

An OLD SECURITY GUARD leers at Derek from outside the court. Derek lets go of Max and gives him a mean look.

> DEREK
> I'll get you later.

Derek and Craig leave. Doug tries to get a grip.

> DOUG
> Wow, that was intense.

INT. SCHRODINGER HOUSE / MAX'S ROOM — NIGHT

Max works on his equations. The numbers come out of his head and fill the room. They are nonsensical and chaotic.

While working on one problem, he gets frustrated. He crosses out the page and throws the pencil.

He rips out the failed equation, crumbles it and throws it away. The crumbled paper hits the numbers, causing them to disappear into a puff of smoke.

Max looks lost, confused.

He looks at Sandy's house. His lights are ON.

EXT. PORCH

Max sneaks out of the house, holding the notebook.

SANDY'S PORCH

Max approaches the DOOR, uncertain of himself. He manages to KNOCK on the door.

> MAX
> Mr. Planck. I mean, Sandy?

> SANDY (O.S.)
> Come in!

Max walks in.

INT. LIVING ROOM

Very under decorated. Nothing but bare necessities.

Sandy prepares food in the kitchen. Max carefully walks in.

                    SANDY
          Can't sleep, huh? Me neither. Take
          a seat.

There are only two chairs around the table. Max sits next to
Alfred. Max pets Alfred, until he notices--

A large red file sitting on the desk. Max approaches it with
curiosity. Right when he is about to look into it--

Sandy grabs the file and puts it in a drawer.

                    SANDY (CONT'D)
          Sorry. Sometimes I leave work
          around. Blueberry Pop Tarts?

Sandy offers the box to Max.

                    MAX
          Sure. They're my favorite actually.

Max slides out a piece from the wrapping.

                    SANDY
          I seem to have misplaced my
          toaster.

                    MAX
          Doesn't matter, I like 'em cold.

They both sit down. Sandy grabs Max's notebook.

                    SANDY
          Let's get this out of the way.

Sandy scribbles for a couple of seconds and gives the
notebook back. Max looks at the notebook. He is shocked.

                    MAX
          How can you do this!?

                    SANDY
          Shhhh. It's a secret. So, how's
          summer treating you?

                    MAX
          Pretty good, I guess. I'm buried in
          work these days.

Max sips on his milk. Sandy shakes his head--

                    SANDY
          How old are you Max?

                    MAX
          Thirteen.

                    SANDY
          Thirteen years old and you sound
          like a fifty-year-old accountant. I
          don't wanna butt into your business
          but if I were you, I'd try to have
          a little bit of what earthlings
          call fun. Once you start O.I.T.,
          you won't have time to wipe your
          ass let alone spend time with
          anyone special.

Max takes a bite out his pop tart.

                    MAX
          Sounds like you're talking from
          experience.

Sandy scoffs. There is an awkward silence.

Albert whimpers in his sleep.

                    MAX (CONT'D)
          How did you find him?

                    SANDY
          I was walking by a street in
          Champaign Illinois when I stopped
          in front of a pet store. I noticed
          this guy sitting alone in a cage.
          He was isolated, away from other
          puppies. At that moment, I knew he
          was the right companion for me.

                    MAX
          So you just walked in and bought
          him? Just like that?

                    SANDY
          Exactly. You see, when something
          feels right, really feels right,
          you just have to act on it no
          matter how crazy or irrational it
          may be. And believe me, it took me
          many years to figure that one out.

                    MAX
          Sandy?

                    SANDY
          Yes Max?

                    MAX
          Would you like to have dinner with
          us tomorrow? You can meet the
          family, check out mom's food…

                    SANDY
          Help with your equations?

                    MAX
          If you want.

Sandy laughs.

                    MAX (CONT'D)
          So, you're coming?

                    SANDY
          Okay. Only if you do me a favor.

                    MAX
          What is it?

                    SANDY
          That thing I said about acting on
          your feelings?

                    MAX
          Yes?

                    SANDY
          I want you to remember that when
          you're buying food for H.G.

Max is confused--

                    MAX
          Okay.

Sandy smiles at Max in reassurance.

INT. EVELYN'S ROOM

Evelyn sleeps.

                    MAX (O.S.)
          Bye Sandy.

                    SANDY (O.S.)
          See you tomorrow.

Evelyn wakes up. She looks outside and notices--

Max walking out of Sandy's house.

She looks worried.

INT. PET STORE — DAY

A relatively small pet store inserted in a line of different
stores at the bottom of the hill.

Max looks at hamster food with H.G.

The nerdy girl from the grocery store enters. A bright light
shines behind her.

Max follows her with his eyes.

The nerdy girl looks at the animals in their cages.

Max passes by the girl. He stops himself. He hesitates for a
while. He takes a deep breath.

Max walks back to the nerdy girl. The anxiety is clearly
readable in his eyes. He stops next to her. He mumbles--

                    MAX
          ...like animals?

The nerdy girl is disoriented.

                    NERDY GIRL
          Sorry?

Max clears his throat too loud, alarming the nerdy girl.

                    MAX
          I meant to ask, you like animals?

                    NERDY GIRL
          Oh yeah. I love them, sometimes
          more than people.

Max observes a hamster in his cage, running on the wheel.

                    MAX
          I know what you mean.

                    NERDY GIRL
          How so?

                    MAX
          You can be whatever you want, say
          whatever you want, and they don't
          expect anything from you.

The nerdy girl is impressed.

                    NERDY GIRL
          Or judge you, tell you what you
          should do or say instead.

                    MAX
          In return, all they need is your
          love and attention. And food.

The nerdy girl laughs. Max's happy he made her laugh.

                    MAX (CONT'D)
          It's all very...

                    NERDY GIRL
          Simple.

                    MAX
          Exactly. Do you have a pet?

                    NERDY GIRL
          No. My dad's against them. He says
          they promote unrealistic
          attachments. So I come here from
          time to time to look.

                    MAX
          Which one's your favorite?

                    NERDY GIRL
          I don't know, hard to pick.

She points to H.G.

                    NERDY GIRL (CONT'D)
          I like hamsters.

Max brings H.G. Closer to the girl.

                    MAX
          This is H.G.

The girl sticks her finger into the cage. HG sniffs it.

                    NERDY GIRL
          Nice to meet you H.G.

                    MAX
          I'm Max.

                    THE NERDY GIRL
          Nice to meet you too.

The Nerdy Girl looks at her watch.

                    THE NERDY GIRL (CONT'D)
          Oh no. I have to go. See you.

The nerdy girl waves and walks toward the door.

                    MAX
          Wait! What's your name?

The nerdy girl stops and turns around.

                    THE NERDY GIRL
          Amanda.

Amanda leaves.

                    MAX
               (to himself)
          Amanda.

INT. SCHRODINGER HOUSE / LIVING ROOM — NIGHT

Evelyn and Chet set up the table. Max walks in from the
kitchen with five plates. Evelyn picks them up.

                    EVELYN
          Why five plates?

                    MAX
          I was wondering if two of my
          friends could join us?

                    CHET
          How did you find two friends?

                    EVELYN
          Chet!

Chet quietly sets the table. Evelyn turns to Max.

                    EVELYN (CONT'D)
          Sure honey. Who are they?

                    MAX
          You know, Doug and...

44.

                              SANDY (O.S.)
                    Hello?

The family looks outside. Sandy is looking at them through
the window with a bag in his hand. He awkwardly waves.

                              MAX
                    ...and Sandy.

Evelyn gets the same oddly familiar, yet off-putting feeling
she had when she first saw Sandy.

                              CHET
                    Wow. He's old.

Evelyn looks worried but tries to hide it from Max.

                              EVELYN
                    I wish you had told me before
                    sweetie. I don't know if we have
                    enough food.

                              CHET
                    Sure we do.

Evelyn makes a sarcastic face to Chet: "Thanks."

Evelyn and Max walk to the door. Chet follows them. Evelyn
opens the door.

                              EVELYN
                    Hi. You must be Sandy.

Sandy is frozen. He's mesmerized by Evelyn's presence.

Evelyn, Max and Chet look at each other, not sure how to
react. Finally, Sandy snaps out of it--

                              SANDY
                    Oh yes! Yes, I am. You must be,
                    Max's mother.

Sandy offers his hand in odd anticipation. Evelyn politely
shakes it.

As soon as they touch, Evelyn is overcome with a familiar
feeling she shouldn't have.

Sandy looks very emotional. He tries his best to hide it.

Chet and Max look at each other: "What's going on?"

As if pulled by an unseen force, Evelyn moves her other hand
to touch Sandy's. Before she can, Sandy pulls his hand away.

                    SANDY (CONT'D)
          I brought Pop Tarts. I didn't have
          anything else, sorry.

Evelyn gets a grip.

                    EVELYN
          Look Max, your favorite. Would you
          like to come in?

                    SANDY
          Sure.

Sandy walks in and Evelyn closes the door.

                                        TIME DISSOLVE

INT. SCHRODINGER HOUSE / LIVING ROOM — NIGHT

The Schrodinger family, Sandy and Doug sit around the dinner
table silently eating their meal.

                    EVELYN
          So, Sandy, Max tells me you're
          quite a genius.

                    SANDY
          Compared to your son, I'm probably
          not that good. You've done a great
          job with him Ms. Schrodinger.

                    EVELYN
          Please, call me Evelyn. So, what
          brings you to Lake Vonnegut?

                    SANDY
          I figured I would take a much
          deserved vacation. You know, to
          relax, take a look at myself in a
          whole new way.

Doug plays with his food. He accidentally drops some on the
floor and acts like nothing happened.

                    EVELYN
          We can always use some of that.
          And what were you doing before, if
          you don't mind me asking?

                    SANDY
          Of course not. I was a technical
          supervisor for I.S.R.O.

46.

                    MAX
          Wow! You worked at The Illinois
          Space Research Organization!?

Evelyn is worried about Max's excitement.

                    EVELYN
          That sounds great.

Evelyn collects the plates.

Doug lifts up his oversized hat to look at Evelyn.

                    DOUG
          Thanks for the meal Ms.
          Schrodinger. It was great.

Evelyn looks at Doug's plate. Doug made a smiley face out of
the food.

                    EVELYN
          Thank you Doug.

Evelyn rolls her eyes and leaves.

EXT. SCHRODINGER HOUSE / PORCH — NIGHT

Sandy stands on the porch sipping a glass of tea.

STREET

Doug and Max run around with Albert.

Albert looks confused as the kids pet him from both sides.

                    DOUG
          Hey Albert, over here!

                    MAX
          No Albert, play with me!

PORCH

Sandy laughs. Chet walks out of the house with a can of beer.

                    SANDY
          Hi there.

Chet approaches Sandy with suspicion.

                    CHET
          So, you're like my brother huh?

                    SANDY
          What do you mean?

                    CHET
          You know, one of those "science is
          my life" kind.

                    SANDY
          You mean "geeks".

                    CHET
          No, I didn't mean…

Sandy faces Chet.

                    SANDY
          Yes you did. You know, it may look
          like the world to you now, being
          accepted by your friends,
          pretending it's no big deal
          whenever they call your brother a
          "freak" so they wouldn't think of
          you as one.

                    CHET
          What!? I never...

Sandy takes a step closer to Chet.

                    SANDY
          But you know what? Those people you
          call friends, none of them have in
          their lives anyone remotely as
          special as Max.

Sandy walks closer to Chet. He whispers.

                    SANDY (CONT'D)
          You might not believe this but your
          brother looks up to you and admires
          you in exactly the same way you are
          secretly admiring him. You may
          think that it's the most obvious
          thing in the world. But it wouldn't
          hurt to let him know, before it's
          too late.

Chet is barely holding on to his beer. Sandy pats Chet on the
shoulder.

                    SANDY (CONT'D)
          Excuse me.

Sandy enters the house. Chet looks deep in thought.

INT. KITCHEN

Evelyn washes the dishes. Sandy stands by the door, unsure if
he should walk in. He decides to go for it.

                    SANDY (O.S.)
          Evelyn?

Evelyn is uncomfortable by Sandy's presence but tries to
focus on the dishes.

                    EVELYN
          Did you enjoy the meal?

                    SANDY
          It was great. Thank you.

                    EVELYN
          You're welcome.

Sandy takes a couple of steps towards Evelyn. Evelyn keeps
her focus on the dishes.

                    SANDY
          Max is a very special boy.

                    EVELYN
          I know.

                    SANDY
          You must love him very much.

Evelyn looks into Sandy's eyes.

                    EVELYN
          More than life itself.

Sandy looks strangely relieved, as if a giant weight is
lifted off his shoulders.

Evelyn doesn't like what she sees. She brakes eye contact.

                    SANDY
          I'm sure he feels the same.

                    EVELYN
          He has a funny way of showing it.

Sandy moves closer to Evelyn.

                    SANDY
          I'm sure he does. He's, just...

Evelyn casually takes a step back as she dries her hands.

                    SANDY (CONT'D)
          Are you okay?

                    EVELYN
          Yes, I'm fine. I just need to clean
          up around here. It's getting late.

Sandy takes a step back.

                    SANDY
          You're right. I better get going as
          well. I…

Suddenly, Sandy's attention shifts to the noise of Max and
Doug playing in the street.

EXT. STREET

Doug and Max run around with Albert.

INT. KITCHEN

Sandy looks very worried.

                    SANDY
          I'm sorry. I...

Sandy dashes out in a hurry.

EXT. STREET

Max sits on the curb, tired. Doug still plays with Albert.

                    DOUG
          Hey Albert! Hey, over here!

Doug runs and trips on the curb. He stumbles across the
street and just when he is about to fall--

A hand grabs Doug before he was about to fall off a steep
hill. Doug looks at the hill below in horror.

Doug gasps and looks back. The hand belongs to Sandy. Evelyn
runs out of the house, startled.

Sandy lifts up Doug. Doug wanders around in shock.

All of a sudden, Sandy has trouble breathing. He starts
coughing. Max looks worried.

Sandy's coughing turns into gasping. He falls on his knees.
Max approaches Sandy with caution.

                    MAX
          Sandy? Are you okay?

Sandy manages to lift his hand, gesturing Max to stand back.

He slowly stops coughing and gains his strength.

He gets up and looks around. Everyone looks at him. He
adjusts himself.

                    SANDY
          I'm sorry I ruined your night.

Sandy stumbles back home. Albert follows him.

Evelyn looks distraught.

INT. SUPERMARKET — DAY

Evelyn and Max walk into an aisle, picking up cleaning
supplies. Rose and Doug at the other end of the aisle. Rose
notices Evelyn.

                    ROSE
          Evelyn!?

                    EVELYN
          Hi Rose.

Rose approaches Evelyn. Doug follows.

                    ROSE
          Isn't it crazy we keep bumping into
          each other?

                    DOUG
          Hi Max.

                    MAX
          Hi.

                    DOUG
          You wanna check out some toys?

                    MAX
          Aren't we a little old for toys?

Doug winks at Max.

                    MAX (CONT'D)
          Huh?

Doug keeps winking in a suggestive way.

                    MAX (CONT'D)
          Fine. I'll be right back mom.

                    EVELYN
          Alright sweetie. Don't get too far.

                    ROSE
          Don't wander off Dougie.

Doug looks annoyed.

                    DOUG
          Alright mom.

TOYS AND GAMES AISLE

Doug sneaks in, imitating a spy. Max casually follows.

                    MAX
          So, what's the big deal?

                    DOUG
          I got the super top secret
          information about your girlfriend.

Doug pretends to look at the toys.

                    MAX
          She's not my girlfriend... Okay,
          what is it?

                    DOUG
          She lives up the hill, a couple of
          cabins away from you.

Doug picks up various toys and pretends to play with them.

                    MAX
          How did you find that out?

                    DOUG
          My mom's files are not exactly
          confidential. She also loves to sit
          by the lake and read. And, her name
          is Amanda.

                    MAX
          I know her name.

Doug drops the toys.

                    DOUG
          How?

52.

                    MAX
          We had a little chat at the pet
          store the other day.

                    DOUG
          Alright man!

Doug turns back to the toys while he walks. Max follows.

                    DOUG (CONT'D)
          I figured I'll follow her around
          and find out her schedule. After
          that, you can find her, pretend
          it's all a coincidence. Then you
          can put on your genius moves.

Doug picks up two action figures--

                    DOUG (CONT'D)
          You can go up to her and be all
          like, "Hey Amanda, you want me to
          show you my algebra skills?"

Doug plays the scene with the toys. Max looks annoyed.

                    DOUG (CONT'D)
          And she'll be like, "Algebra!? I
          love algebra!".

Doug makes the toys kiss and does smooching sounds.

Max knocks the figures off of Doug's hand.

                    MAX
          Stop that!

                    DOUG
          Sorry. So, what do you think?

                    MAX
          Great plan.

                    DOUG
          You bet. And if anyone finds out
          I'm following her, you can pretend
          you don't know me.

                    MAX
          I'm already doing that anyway.

                    DOUG
          Ha ha. Funny.

PRODUCE AISLE

Rose and Evelyn peruse around.

                    ROSE
          Did you meet anyone else around the
          lake yet?

                    EVELYN
          Well, not really. Oh, we did meet
          our next door neighbor.

Rose picks up some vegetables, looks at them for a while and puts them in the wrong place. Evelyn follows her.

                    ROSE
          I know. Sandy. What do you think
          about him?

                    EVELYN
          I'm not sure. My son likes him.

                    ROSE
          I'm not sure either. Don't get me
          wrong. I'm grateful to him for
          saving my son. But doesn't he seem
          kind of, you know, weird?

Evelyn looks hypnotized.

                    EVELYN
          Yes. I mean, why do you think so?

Rose stops looking at the vegetables and turns to Evelyn.

                    ROSE
          He came to me to buy that cabin
          next to yours, specifically that
          cabin, about a month ago. He put up
          a lot of money for it too. Much
          above its usual price.

                    EVELYN
          So? Maybe he loved the place?

                    ROSE
          Maybe.
                    (whispering)
          But I wanted to find out more about
          him. For, you know, security
          reasons. I couldn't find a single
          file on this man, apart from the
          documents he showed me when he
          bought the place.
                    (MORE)

                    ROSE (CONT'D)
          He had all the necessary papers
          with him. But when I did some
          research on him on the web, I
          couldn't find anything.

Evelyn seems intrigued but tries to hide it.

                    EVELYN
          He used to work at I.S.R.O. People
          who work there, they tend not to be
          very social, especially with all
          the classified work they do.

Rose is not convinced.

                    ROSE
          Maybe you're right. Why do you
          think he's weird?

                    EVELYN
          I didn't say he's weird.

                    ROSE
          Right, you didn't. Come on, I'm
          your friend. You can tell me.

Evelyn's torn. She doesn't know how to fully explain--

                    EVELYN
          There's something about him that
          feels... Very close and, familiar,
          yet, at the same time, cold and
          distant. Like a long forgotten
          dream that always lives somewhere
          inside you. I feel this intense
          attraction to him, but not in the
          way you'd think. He frightens me.

                    ROSE
          Why? You said you're not attracted
          to him in that way.

                    EVELYN
          That's exactly why he scares me.
          It's his eyes. His eyes are...

Evelyn snaps out of her daze.

                    EVELYN (CONT'D)
          Look at me, talking like this about
          someone I don't even know.

> ROSE
> I guess we won't ever know who he
> really is.

Evelyn comes up with an idea--

> EVELYN
> That's not necessarily true.

Rose looks intrigued.

EXT. LAKE — DAY

Moderately crowded. Doug sneaks out behind a tree like an awkward James Bond.

He pulls out his binoculars and looks through--

--INSERT - BINOCULARS POV

Amanda swims by herself. The binoculars turn to a bench with a pink date book on it.

--BACK TO SCENE

Doug jumps to the ground. He rolls around and leans next to the bench. He checks the area to make sure no one is looking and grabs the date book.

The pages on the book are mostly empty, except for 'Swimming and reading' written next to 6 AM on each page. Doug smiles.

INT. SCHRODINGER HOUSE / MAX'S ROOM — NIGHT

Max works on his projects.

A knock on the door. Evelyn enters with the phone.

> EVELYN
> It's Doug.

Max picks up the phone. Evelyn leaves.

> MAX
> *(imitating Rose)*
> Hi Dougie.

> DOUG (ON PHONE)
> Please don't do that. I got the
> perfect idea for you to spend some
> quality time with Amanda.

> MAX
> Really?

Max drops his pencil and gives Doug his full attention.

> DOUG (ON PHONE)
> She likes to swim every day at six
> in the morning. There will be no
> one at the lake that early.

> MAX
> I guess.

> DOUG (ON PHONE)
> Are you gonna do it?

> MAX
> I don't know.

> DOUG (ON PHONE)
> Come on man! This could be your
> only chance.

> MAX
> Alright, I'll try.

> DOUG (ON PHONE)
> Awesome man!

> MAX
> *(imitating Rose)*
> Bye Dougie.

> DOUG (ON PHONE)
> I'm telling you for the last time.
> Stop calling me...

Max hangs up the phone. He sits on the bed and sighs.

After thinking for a while, he picks up the alarm clock and sets it to "5:30".

He puts the alarm clock back on the table.

TIME DISSOLVE - DAY

The alarm clock shows "5:29". It hits "5:30" and RINGS.

Max opens his eyes and gets up. He sits on the bed, trying to wake up.

> MAX
> I can't do this.

He turns off the alarm and lays back on the bed. He is startled by a glass noise.

Max looks up. A pebble hits the window. He gets up and looks outside.

Sandy stands on the porch, holding a handful of pebbles. Alfred sits next to him.

Sandy waves casually at Max. Max looks confused.

EXT. PORCH

Max walks out.

> SANDY
> How are you?

> MAX
> Okay, I guess. What's going on?

> SANDY
> I had some trouble sleeping so I
> figured I'd just drop by.

> MAX
> At five thirty in the morning?

> SANDY
> You weren't doing anything
> important were you?

Sandy sits on the ground outside. Max sits next to him.

> MAX
> I was sleeping. At least I was
> trying to sleep.

> SANDY
> Are you sure?

> MAX
> I guess I'm supposed to be
> somewhere right now.

> SANDY
> Really? Where?

> MAX
> I can't tell you.

> SANDY
> Tell me now or I'll have Albert
> torture you.

Max looks at Albert. Albert yawns and plops his body on the ground. Max and Sandy laugh.

58.

                    MAX
          It's just this stupid thing.
          Totally unimportant.

Sandy focuses on the beautiful view of the sunrise--

                    SANDY
          Funny thing about stupid,
          unimportant things. After the day
          is done, it's those unimportant
          moments that seem to get stuck in
          your mind.

                    MAX
          What do you mean?

                    SANDY
          When I was younger, I used to work
          non-stop for days. Sometimes, I'd
          put on music to keep me company.
          Other times, I'd keep the TV on
          some random channel. It didn't
          matter which one, as long as it
          quieted my mind. I used to look at
          those commercials with people
          walking happily along some sunny
          beach. And there I was, stuck in
          some lab, in a God forsaken
          basement, in the middle of nowhere.

                    MAX
          Why didn't you get out?

                    SANDY
          I wanted to. I wanted to do a lot
          of things. But time is tricky.
          First you think you have a lot of
          it. Then you realize you never
          really had any.

Max looks thoughtful. He looks determined and focused.

                    MAX
          Sandy, can I...

                    SANDY
          Of course you can go.

                    MAX
          What about you?

                    SANDY
          Albert will keep me company.

Albert is still sleeping. Max smiles.

> MAX
> Thank you.

> SANDY
> Enjoy it kid.

Max runs off, excited. Sandy looks after him with pride.

EXT. LAKE — DAY

Max looks at Amanda, swimming by herself.

The light of the dawning sun glitters on the water as she swims elegantly through it.

Max stands behind the tree next to the lake. He watches Amanda in amazement.

Amanda swims out of the lake and dries herself. As she dries her hair, she notices Max. She's startled--

> AMANDA
> Who's there?

Max comes out from behind the tree.

> AMANDA (CONT'D)
> Max?

> MAX
> You remembered my name.

> AMANDA
> What are you doing here so early?

> MAX
> I just felt like taking a walk.
> How about you?

Max shyly approaches Amanda.

> AMANDA
> I always come down here when
> there's no one around. I like it
> better that way.

> MAX
> Sorry. I'll leave you alone.

Max turns to leave.

                    AMANDA
          That's okay. You can stay.

Max turns back.

                    AMANDA (CONT'D)
          Organic dried fruit?

Max searches for the right answer.

                    MAX
          Sure.

Amanda sits on a bench and dries her hair. Max sits on the
other side of the bench.

He bites on a piece of dried fruit. He chews the rubbery
fruit with all his might.

There's an awkward silence. Max picks up Amanda's iPod.

                    MAX (CONT'D)
          May I?

                    AMANDA
          Sure.

Max looks through Amanda's albums.

                    MAX
          You like The Animals?

                    AMANDA
          Didn't you ask me that before? I
          said yes.

                    MAX
          No, I mean the band. "House of the
          Rising Sun", "Don't Let Me Be
          Misunderstood."

                    AMANDA
          I know what you meant, I was just
          playing. I love them.

Max smiles.

                    AMANDA (CONT'D)
          You didn't bring your little friend
          with you.

Max is surprised at himself.

                    MAX
          You're right. I didn't.

A couple more silent seconds pass.

                    AMANDA
          What are you doing at Vonnegut?

                    MAX
          The last vacation of my life.

                    AMANDA
          Why do you say that?

                    MAX
          I'm heading to O.I.T. this year.

Amanda picks up two colorful strings of wool.

                    AMANDA
          Wow, O.I.T. huh? That's big. You
          must be some kind of genius.

                    MAX
          Yeah, I guess.

                    AMANDA
          What kind of stuff are you gonna
          work on?

                    MAX
          Things people can't even believe
          exists. I'm working on something
          right now. Something very big.

                    AMANDA
          Cool. What is it?

                    MAX
          Shhhh. It's a secret.

Amanda smiles.

                    AMANDA
          Fair enough.

                    MAX
          How about you? What will you do?

                    AMANDA
          I wanna be one of those lawyers who
          only takes free cases.

62.

                    MAX
          Okay. How will you make money?

Amanda pulls out a bunch of wool out of her bag.

                    AMANDA
          I make wool bracelets.

                    MAX
          Okay.

                    AMANDA
          Do you want one?

                    MAX
          Sure.

Amanda ties a blue bracelet on Max's arm.

                    AMANDA
          You know, these are going to be
          worth a lot someday.

                    MAX
          How?

                    AMANDA
          If you go on TV for inventing a new
          rocket ship or something, I'll tell
          everyone "Hey! I used to know that
          guy. He's wearing my bracelet!"
          It'll be famous and I'll make a lot
          of money.

                    MAX
          Used to? How do you know we won't
          be friends then?

                    AMANDA
          You did say this is your last
          vacation. I bet that goes for
          having friends in the future.

                    MAX
          We still have the rest of summer.
          And I can still feel like taking a
          walk at six in the morning.

                    AMANDA
          If you do, I'll be right here.

Max smiles. Amanda looks at her watch.

                    AMANDA (CONT'D)
          I have to go.

Amanda picks up her stuff.

                    AMANDA (CONT'D)
          See you later.

                    MAX
          Okay. Bye.

Amanda runs off. Max is speechless.

EXT. FOREST — DAY

Max struts through the trees with an inerasable smile.

A hand pushes him to the ground. Max turns around. Derek and
Craig stand over him.

                    DEREK
          I told you I'd find you.

Craig grabs Max by his shirt and lifts him up. Max looks
scared. He turns away.

Craig lifts his fist. Before he can land it, it's stopped by
another hand.

Craig turns around. The hand belongs to Sandy.

Sandy pushes Craig at Derek. They both stumble back.

                    DEREK (CONT'D)
          Who the hell are you!?

Sandy grabs Derek and looks at him straight in the eyes.

                    SANDY
          The last person you'll see if you
          don't leave him alone.

Craig and Derek reluctantly run off. Sandy turns around and
helps Max up.

                    SANDY (CONT'D)
          Come on. I'll take you home.

Max and Sandy walk back home.

                    MAX
          How did you know I was here?

64.

                    SANDY
          I didn't. I just felt like going
          for a hike.

Max and Sandy walk for a while in complete silence.

                    SANDY (CONT'D)
          So are you going to tell me what
          happened or do I have to wait a
          decade or two?

                    MAX
          Just a couple of jerks who were
          messing with me and Doug.

                    SANDY
          I'm not talking about them.

Sandy winks at Max.

                    MAX
          Oh yeah. It was, okay.

                    SANDY
          Come on, don't be so modest.

                    MAX
          Okay, it was great. It was the
          greatest moment of my life. Are you
          happy? For her it was probably just
          a waste of time with some weird kid
          but for me, it was amazing.

                    SANDY
          A moment you will probably remember
          for the rest of your life. Don't
          believe that Amanda thinks of you
          as just some weird kid. I bet she
          likes you as much as you like her.
          No asshole bullies, Mikes or Ricks
          can change that fact.

Max is disoriented.

                    MAX
          How do you know her name?

                    SANDY
          Who?

                    MAX
          Amanda. How did you know her name?
          Did Doug tell you?

                    SANDY
          No.

                    MAX
          Okay, I want to know right now.
          How do you know these things!?

Sandy starts sweating.

                    SANDY
          Come to think of it, I think it was
          Doug who told me.

                    MAX
          You're lying, I can tell. Something
          happened to you, didn't it? At the
          institute, they did something to
          you, didn't they!?

                    SANDY
          I'm sorry, I just, I just can't
          tell you... I… Oh no.

Sandy coughs, gasping for his life.

                    MAX
          Sandy!? Sandy, are you okay!?

Sandy stumbles and gasps for air. He sits on a tree stump. He
wheezes in and out, trying to breathe.

Max is in a state of shock. He doesn't know what to do and
can barely move. Sandy hardly manages to speak.

                    SANDY
          Do you really want to know who I
          am? I'm a ghost.

Sandy diverts his eyes away from Max.

                    SANDY (CONT'D)
          I turned my back to all who cared
          about me and now I'm paying the
          price for it. I don't even exist.
          But you, you have your entire life
          ahead of you.

Sandy coughs, then gets a grip. Max watches him, helpless.

                    SANDY (CONT'D)
          Don't make the same mistakes I did.
          Hold onto the people you care about
          the most and don't let go of them
          no matter what.

Max looks affected by Sandy's speech. Sandy tries to regain some of his strength.

                SANDY (CONT'D)
    Let's go home.

Max helps Sandy up and the two continue walking home.

INT. SCHRODINGER HOUSE / KITCHEN — DAY

Evelyn stands in the middle of the kitchen with a business card in one hand and her phone in the other.

After thinking whether or not she's making the right choice, she dials a number--

                EVELYN
    Hello, Nick? Nick Sullivan?

NICK, 40, talks on the other line.

                NICK (ON PHONE)
    Yes?

                EVELYN
    Hi, this is Evelyn Schrodinger. I
    gave a seminar at your company. You
    had problems with managing your
    workload and I helped you out?

                NICK (ON PHONE)
    Oh yes, of course. I can't thank
    you enough for that.

                EVELYN
    You're welcome. I don't feel good
    about asking you this but... Do you
    remember you told me that if I
    needed your help with anything, to
    call you no matter what?

                NICK (ON PHONE)
    Sure.

Evelyn walks around, unsure of what she's about to do.

                EVELYN
    I have a big favor to ask.

                NICK (ON PHONE)
    Go ahead.

                EVELYN
    Your wife still works for I.S.R.O?

                    NICK (ON PHONE)
          Yes.

                    EVELYN
          How high up is she?

                    NICK (ON PHONE)
          Pretty high up.

                    EVELYN
          Can you ask her to look up someone
          who used to work there?

EXT. STREET

Sandy and Max walk up to the house.

INT. KITCHEN

                    EVELYN
          Thank you Nick. Bye.

Evelyn hangs up and looks outside the window.

Sandy waves at Max and walks to his house. Max waves back.

Evelyn looks worried.

EXT. LAKE - DAY

Early morning hours. The dawning sun shines on the lake.

Max and Amanda sit on a towel by the calm water, looking at
each other's iPod play lists.

                    MAX
          Wow, you're hard core. You even
          have the later Eric Burdon stuff.

                    AMANDA
          Not as hard core as you. Look at
          all these bootlegs. How did you get
          your digital hands on these?

                    MAX
          I'll tell you on one condition.

Amanda's game.

                    AMANDA
          What is it?

                              MAX
                    Hang out with me and, maybe my
                    weird friend, later today? We can
                    play some ball.

                              AMANDA
                    Basketball? Are you good at it?

                              MAX
                    Not even a little bit.

Amanda laughs. Max joins her.

                              AMANDA
                    Sure, I'll be there.

Max is in the clouds. Amanda looks at the inviting lake.

                              AMANDA (CONT'D)
                    I wanna swim. Do you wanna join?

                              MAX
                    I don't know. It looks cold.

Amanda holds Max's hand.

                              AMANDA
                    Come on.

Max's blushing. He tries to hide it.

                              MAX
                    Okay.

Amanda runs into the water. She screams with joy as her body
splashes into the lake.

Max is shy. As he looks at Amanda enjoying herself, carefree,
he takes off his shirt and jumps into the water.

He swims to Amanda. They laugh as they swim around each
other.

Suddenly, the laughter stops. They look into each other's
eyes, in silence. They're falling in love.

Amanda splashes water on Max's face. She laughs and swims
away. Max swims after her for revenge.

Max catches up to Amanda and splashes water on her face. They
play like children under the tranquility of nature.

EXT. CAMP SITE — NIGHT

A bunch of TEENAGERS drink, talk and have fun around a camp fire, surrounded by the mysterious trees.

Chet sits on the ground, chatting with Bonnie (MOS).

MIKE, 18, cocky, approaches Chet.

> MIKE
> Hey Chet.

Chet turns to Mike.

> MIKE (CONT'D)
> You want another beer?

> CHET
> I can't man. I have to head back
> soon or mom will kill me.

> MIKE
> What's the matter with your mom,
> man? Is she forcing you to read
> bedtime stories to your autistic
> brother or something?

Chet is offended. Mike's friends laugh.

Mike turns to his friend.

> MIKE (CONT'D)
> Did you see his brother with that
> geek Doug? They're a perfect match.

Mike's friends laugh. Chet gets up and confronts Mike.

> CHET
> Don't say another word about Max.

Mike looks stunned.

> MIKE
> What?

> CHET
> I said, don't talk about my brother
> like that.

Mike gets up and confronts Chet.

> MIKE
> And what if I do?

                    CHET
          You'll regret it.

Mike laughs.

                    MIKE
          I wouldn't expect a dumbass move
          like that from you. I guess the
          apple doesn't fall far from the
          retarded tree.

Mike gets uncomfortably close to Chet.

                    MIKE (CONT'D)
          You're a freak like your brother.

Chet punches Mike. Mike falls to the ground.

                    CHET
          I'm the freak who's still standing.

Chet turns to leave. Mike jumps up, screaming in anger. He
hits Chet in the back.

Chet turns around and punches Mike. There's pandemonium. The
kids tries to pull them apart as the two fight violently.

INT. SCHRODINGER HOUSE / LIVING ROOM — NIGHT

Max scribbles on his notebook. He works on the schematic for
the octagon-shaped machine.

                    EVELYN (O.S.)
          I guess this is some progress.

Max folds the schematic and puts it away.

                    MAX
          What is?

Evelyn sits across Max with a cup of coffee.

                    EVELYN
          At least you came out of your room.

Max smiles.

                    EVELYN (CONT'D)
          I'm so glad we came here. This
          place finally opened you up a bit.

                    MAX
          Strange. That's what Sandy says.

Evelyn looks thoughtful.

                    EVELYN
          Listen, sweetie. About Sandy…

Max looks behind Evelyn. He looks startled.

                    MAX
          Chet?

Evelyn turns around. Chet stands at the doorway with bruises
on his face. Bonnie helps him stand.

Evelyn and Max get up to help him.

                    CHET
          You should see the other guy.

                    EVELYN
          What the hell happened!?

Evelyn and Max help Chet to the couch.

                    BONNIE
          He had a fight.

                    EVELYN
          I can see that!

                    CHET
          Mom, my ears are still ringing. I
          don't need you to add to that.

Evelyn helps Chet into the kitchen. Max stays with Bonnie.

                    BONNIE
          You two must be really close.

Max looks surprised.

                    MAX
          Not really.

                    BONNIE
          That's weird.

                    MAX
          What do you mean?

                    BONNIE
          He got into the fight because of
          you. Some kid called you names and
          he jumped him. I wish my brother
          would stand up for me like that.

Max looks speechless.

> BONNIE (CONT'D)
> I have to go. Tell him to call me
> if he needs anything.

Max nods. Bonnie walks out.

INT. KITCHEN - NIGHT

Max walks in. Chet's leaning on a chair with an ice pack on his head.

> CHET
> How's it going, little man?

> MAX
> Thank you.

> CHET
> For what?

Max smiles. Chet smiles back.

> CHET (CONT'D)
> No problem.

Evelyn walks in. She switches the ice packs. Chet moans.

> EVELYN
> You better tell me what happened if
> you want to even think about going
> out for the rest of the vacation!
> You got that!?

Chet looks at Max and sighs.

> CHET
> It's gonna be a long summer.

Max laughs. Chet joins him.

BEGIN MONTAGE -- PASSING OF TIME

--Max and Amanda play by the lake (MOS) at early morning. Max laughs. Amanda smiles innocently at Max.

--Chet rows with his friends.

--Max introduces Amanda to Doug at the common area. Doug gives Amanda an unexpected hug. Amanda hugs him back.

--Max and Sandy work on Max's projects on Sandy's porch. Max throws away pages, frustrated. Sandy calms him down.

--Evelyn types in Sandy's name on a search engine. The screen reads "No Results Found." Evelyn looks worried.

--Amanda and Max exchange CDs at the mountainside. Max pulls out a CD-R from his pocket. Amanda jumps in excitement and hugs Max. Max smiles.

--Amanda, Max and Doug bike alongside the forest. Doug tries a 'no hands' stunt and falls off his bike.

--Max and Amanda drink lemonade on Sandy's porch. They smile at each other.

--Max and Amanda run around with Albert at the lake. They throw a ball for him to catch. Albert looks at where the ball went and decides to sleep instead.

EXT. FOREST — DAY

Max, Amanda and Doug walk side by side. Doug wears fifteen wool bracelets on each arm.

                    AMANDA
          Doug, I'm glad you like my
          bracelets, but you don't have to
          wear all of them.

                    DOUG
          It's cool. I like them.

Doug looks at his WATCH.

                    DOUG (CONT'D)
          I gotta go home.

Doug winks at Max and suggestively points at Amanda. Max gestures at Doug: 'Stop that.'

Doug runs off. Amanda waves at Doug.

Max and Amanda resume walking.

                    AMANDA
          Max?

                    MAX
          Yes?

                    AMANDA
          Do you think I'm pretty?

Max gulps.

                         AMANDA (CONT'D)
               I'm just asking because you said
               you look at everything in a
               scientific way. What do you see
               when you look at me? Am I a good-
               looking girl?

Max looks carefully at Amanda's face. He savors being able to
look at her for so long.

                         MAX
               In strictly scientific terms,
               everything's as imperfect as they
               can be. The alignment between the
               right and left side of your face
               are off. Your nose is too small in
               proportion to your eyes. The right
               side of your mouth is tilted up at
               an odd angle.

Amanda is hurt by Max's comments.

                         MAX (CONT'D)
               But somehow, it's all of those
               imperfections that make you
               absolutely... Perfect.

Amanda smiles. Her eyes well with tears.

They continue walking.

                         MAX (CONT'D)
               I have to talk to you about
               something. You know how we are good
               friends now?

                         AMANDA
               Yeah?

                         MAX
               Have you ever… Have you ever
               thought about…

                         RICK (O.S.)
               Hey Amanda!

Max turns around. It's RICK CARVER, 15, athletic and good-
looking. He's in full river rafting gear.

Amanda turns red as soon as she notices Rick.

                         AMANDA
               Hi Rick. What's up?

                    RICK
          Headin' down to the river for some
          rafting. We missed you yesterday at
          the lake. Where were you?

                    AMANDA
          I was just, around.

Max sneers at Rick. He looks intimidated.

                    RICK
          Cool. See you later.

Rick casually waves at Max and walks off.

                    AMANDA
          Bye. Oh my god!

                    MAX
          Who was that?

                    AMANDA
          Rick Carver. He's awesome at
          everything. Rafting, kayaking,
          basketball. He's so cool!

Max looks annoyed.

                    AMANDA (CONT'D)
          Are you okay? You look weird.

                    MAX
          No, I'm okay. I just have to go
          home. I'll see you later.

Max walks away.

                    AMANDA
          Max. I, it wasn't...

                    MAX
          It's cool, see you later.

Amanda tries to speak but stops herself. She walks off the
other way.

Max looks distraught. He kicks the leaves in anger.

INT. SCHRODINGER HOUSE / LIVING ROOM — NIGHT

Evelyn is preparing salad. She chops up some lettuce.

Her phone rings, she picks it up.

                         EVELYN
              Hello?

The voice of CAROL, 40, is heard.

                         CAROL (ON PHONE)
              Ms. Schrodinger?

                         EVELYN
              Yes?

                         CAROL (ON PHONE)
              Hi, I'm Carol Sullivan. You talked
              to my husband about a Sandy Planck?

Evelyn stops chopping and listens intently.

                         EVELYN
              Oh yes.

                         CAROL (ON PHONE)
              I looked into our records. No one
              by that name has ever worked with
              us. There is no one in our records
              that match your description of him.

                         EVELYN
              I see. Thank you.

Evelyn turns off the phone.

                         SANDY (O.S.)
              Max?

Evelyn looks outside. Sandy stands on the porch.

EXT. PORCH

Evelyn approaches Sandy with determination.

                         SANDY
              Hi Evelyn. Is Max in? We were
              supposed to work on his projects.

                         EVELYN
              I have to talk to you.

                         SANDY
              What's wrong?

Evelyn takes a step toward Sandy but keeps her distance.

                         EVELYN
              I don't want you to see my son.

                    SANDY
          Why?

                    EVELYN
          I don't know who you are Sandy. We
          don't know who you are.

                    SANDY
          What do you mean? You know me. I
          told you, I'm...

                    EVELYN
          I know what you told us. That's not
          the problem. I checked your name
          with high ranking people at
          I.S.R.O. They told me they never
          even heard of you.

Evelyn confronts Sandy while Sandy steps back.

                    EVELYN (CONT'D)
          They don't have any files or
          records on you. In fact, I can't
          find any information about you
          anywhere. It's like, you don't even
          exist. How can you expect me to
          trust you with Max when you've been
          lying to us from the start?

Sandy thinks very hard about whether or not to say--

                    SANDY
          Because you wouldn't believe me if
          I told you the truth.

                    EVELYN
          Don't presume what I will and will
          not believe!

Sandy holds Evelyn's hands. There's electricity between them.

                    SANDY
          I'm sorry. I'm so sorry. For
          everything that I've done.

Sandy tries to hug Evelyn. Evelyn pushes Sandy away.

                    EVELYN
          Get away from me! What the hell is
          wrong with you!?

Sandy stumbles back. He is in tears from Evelyn's rejection.

                         SANDY
               I'm sorry, I'm sorry.

Evelyn looks into Sandy's eyes and is deeply concerned for
her sorrow. Finally, she averts her gaze from Sandy.

                         EVELYN
               Who are you?

                         SANDY
               I can't tell you! I…

Sandy coughs and gasps in pain. He leans on the wall. He
tries to gain his strength.

Evelyn watches him in fear but holds herself together.

                         EVELYN
               I want you to stay away from me and
               my family.

Sandy manages to nod through the pain. Sandy reluctantly
leaves, still breathing heavily.

Evelyn sighs. She turns to notice--

Max standing next to the entrance. He looks mad.

                         EVELYN (CONT'D)
               Sweetie, I'm sorry. I…

Max furiously passes by Evelyn.

                         MAX
               Leave me alone!

Evelyn holds Max's arm.

                         EVELYN
               Honey, I'm sorry.

Max pulls himself away.

                         MAX
               Don't touch me! You always have to
               keep me away from what I want,
               don't you!? Nothing I do is good
               enough for you!!

                         EVELYN
               That's not true.

                         MAX
               Tell that to dad.

Max runs in the house and slams the door.

Evelyn sits on the ground. Hopeless, she begins to cry.

INT. MAX'S ROOM - NIGHT

Max scribes equations and formulas with haste. The numbers
fly off of the page and crash into each other, as if they are
in battle.

He cries his eyes out. He harshly crosses out a page and
moves on to the next one.

He crosses out his next equation and moves on. Frustrated, he
throws the notebook away, scaring H.G.

There's a knock on the entrance door.

Max looks outside. It's Doug, holding a basketball.

EXT. PORCH

Max slightly opens the door and peeks out.

                    MAX
          What do you want Doug?

                    DOUG
          Are you alright?

                    MAX
          I'm fine. What do you want?

                    DOUG
          I was just wondering if you wanted
          to play.

                    MAX
          I can't. Leave me alone.

                    DOUG
          Dude, what's wrong?

Max opens the door and confronts Doug.

                    MAX
          Can't you take a hint!? I don't
          wanna be your friend! Nobody wants
          to be your friend! Go away!

Doug tries to hold back on his tears.

                    DOUG
          Max, I…

                    MAX
          If you'll excuse me, I have a lot
          of work to do.

Max closes the door. Doug stands on the porch with teary
eyes. He reluctantly leaves.

INT. MAX'S ROOM - NIGHT

Max rips off pages and throws them away.

Max looks exhausted and frustrated. The floor is filled with
discarded paper.

He rips off another page and stops himself. He looks out of
the window. He looks hopeless.

                              MATCH DISSOLVE
                              TO:

**INT. OLD SCHRODINGER APARTMENT / YOUNG MAX'S ROOM — NIGHT
(FLASHBACK)**

YOUNG MAX, 7, sits at the edge of his bed. He looks at the
window, sad and confused. Rain drops hit the window.

                    PHILIP (O.S.)
          Can't you see I have to do this!?

                    EVELYN (O.S.)
          You're just going to leave us all
          behind!? Just like that!?

Young Max writes math problems on his notebook, trying to
shut out the fight.

                    PHILIP (O.S.)
          This is my life!!

                    EVELYN (O.S.)
          Alright, have it your way! But if
          you leave now, don't ever think
          about coming back!

Young Max tries to keep himself from crying. There's a knock
on the door. Philip enters.

                    PHILIP
          Max? Are you okay?

Philip sits on the bed, close to Young Max.

                    YOUNG MAX
          Yes, I think.

                    PHILIP
          Listen Max. You may not like what I
          am about to say. But in time, you
          will understand.

Young Max puts down the notebook and looks at Philip.

                    YOUNG MAX
          What's wrong dad?

Philip holds Young Max.

                    PHILIP
          Max, I have to go away for a while.
          In fact, I might not be back for a
          long time.

Young Max starts crying.

                    YOUNG MAX
          Why?

                    PHILIP
          I was chosen for a long research
          trip, by some very important
          people. I'll be working on things
          people can't even begin to imagine.
          If it goes right, I'll be more
          successful than I thought possible.

Young Max seems too distraught to speak. Philip looks at
Young Max's notebook.

                    PHILIP (CONT'D)
          Did you work on your problems?

Young Max halfheartedly nods. Philip looks at what Young Max
had written.

                    PHILIP (CONT'D)
          This is amazing. You really are
          your father's son.

Philip gives the notebook back to Young Max. He looks at him
straight in the eye.

                    PHILIP (CONT'D)
          Make me proud.

Young Max wipes off his tears.

                    YOUNG MAX
          Okay dad.

A car horn is heard from outside.

> PHILIP
> I have to go.

> YOUNG MAX
> Dad...

Philip kisses Young Max on the forehead.

> PHILIP
> Goodbye son.

Philip leaves. Young Max runs to the window.

EXT. CITY STREET

Philip mounts a red car. It drives off.

A MAN wearing a hooded coat stands next to the car and watches it as it drives away.

INT. YOUNG MAX'S ROOM

Young Max closes the curtain and sits on a chair. He looks at his notebook. He picks it up. He starts writing.

> MATCH DISSOLVE
> TO:

INT. MAX'S ROOM — NIGHT (PRESENT TIME)

Max writes on his notebook. He stares at a stack of papers filled with math problems, sprawled out over the table.

There is a knock on the door. The door opens and Evelyn sticks out her head.

> EVELYN
> Max?

Max speaks without turning around.

> MAX
> What do you want mom?

Evelyn walks in.

> EVELYN
> I'm sorry.

Evelyn sits next to Max.

                    EVELYN (CONT'D)
          If you want to spend time with
          Sandy, go ahead.

                    MAX
          I can't spend time with anyone
          these days, mom. I have to work.
          But that doesn't make me good
          enough, does it?

Evelyn sighs. She puts her hand on Max's shoulder.

                    EVELYN
          Max, I'm your mother and I love
          you. I will love you no matter what
          you do. Whether you decide to do
          nothing but work and push away
          everyone around you or just choose
          to let go of it all, and live like
          a bum, I will still love you more
          than anything in the world.

Evelyn has tears in his eyes. Max tries to ignore her.

                    EVELYN (O.S.) (CONT'D)
          I'll be perfectly happy with
          whatever you decide to do as long
          as that decision makes you happy.
          Even if that means I have to leave
          you alone for the rest of your
          life. Even if I have to let you go
          somewhere far away, knowing I will
          never see you again. I'll do it.
          As long as I know you are happy.

Max hugs Evelyn as tight as he can--

                    MAX
          I don't want you to leave me mom.
          I don't want you to ever leave me.
          I love you.

Evelyn starts crying.

                    EVELYN
          I love you too sweetie.

Evelyn lets go of Max.

                    EVELYN (CONT'D)
          Now get back to work, if that's
          what you want.

Max nods. Evelyn kisses Max's forehead and leaves.

Max looks back at his papers. He writes with inspiration.

                                        MATCH DISSOLVE
                                        TO:

Max sleeps on the desk, still grasping his pen.

A scratching sound. Max awakes. He looks outside.

Albert waits on the porch with a thick file in his mouth. He looks at Max's room.

EXT. PORCH

Max opens the door. He walks toward Albert.

                    MAX
          Hey Albert. What's that?

Albert leaves the file on the ground.

Max picks the file up and opens it. It's filled with documents with complex math and science problems.

He looks at the first page. It reads--

"Max: In these papers you will find the solutions for all of the problems we've been working on. These should hold you for the summer".

There's a note at the bottom:

"P.S: Remember, The smallest things in life are the most important. The rest is just paper".

Max turns to Sandy's house.

Sandy stands on his porch, looking at Max with pride.

Sandy waves at Max. Max waves back. They both smile at each other in reassurance.

EXT. DOUG'S HOUSE / PORCH — NIGHT

Max knocks on the door. Doug answers.

                    DOUG
          What are you doing here? It's two
          in the morning.

                    ROSE (O.S.)
          Who is it Dougie!?

                    DOUG
          It's cool mom! It's just Max!

Doug turns back to Max.

                    DOUG (CONT'D)
          What do you want?

                    MAX
          I'm sorry about what I said. I
          didn't mean it.

                    DOUG
          Really?

                    MAX
          Yes. Can you forgive me?

Doug thinks for a while.

                    DOUG
          Sure. What are friends for?

Max smiles.

                    MAX
          Exactly.

Doug looks full of happiness.

                    DOUG
          Do you wanna come in?

INT. DOUG'S LIVING ROOM - NIGHT

Doug and Max sit around the table, eating peanut butter and
jelly sandwiches.

                    DOUG
          How are things with Amanda?

                    MAX
          Bad. Turns out she has a crush on
          this kid.

                    DOUG
          Really? Who?

                    MAX
          Rick Carver.

                    DOUG
          Wow, you're screwed dude.

                    MAX
          Thanks for the support. I don't
          know what to do.

                    DOUG
          You can't give up that easy.
          There's a big party next week at
          the community gathering site. You
          can tell her there how you feel.

Doug pulls off pieces from his sandwich. He makes the pieces
dance romantically.

                    DOUG (CONT'D)
          Romantic music. Warm fireside. A
          sea of stars. It's perfect.

Large chunks of jelly drip on the table. Doug picks it up
with his finger and licks it off.

                    MAX
          But how will I tell her? It needs
          to be something big.

                    DOUG
          I dunno, you're the genius. Just
          come up with something.

                    MAX
          I can't.

                    DOUG
          Just think to yourself. What are
          you best at?

Max thinks for a while. He smiles.

INT. DOUG'S ROOM - NIGHT

A rough schematic of the gathering site hits the table.

                    DOUG
          For this to work, we have to get
          the timing just right.

Doug's room is chaotic and larger than life.

                    MAX
          Why do we need a plan of the site?

                    DOUG
          To make this whole thing look
          cooler than it actually is.

Max looks clueless.

> DOUG (CONT'D)
> The band will play right there. I
> think we can use their power supply
> so that shouldn't be a problem.

> MAX
> Will the band let us do that?

> DOUG
> I doubt it.

Doug looks back at the plan.

> DOUG (CONT'D)
> Moving on! Hmmm…

> MAX
> What?

> DOUG
> We have to make you look cool too.
> A little more stylish. Do you know
> anyone who can help us?

EXT. SCHRODINGER HOUSE - NIGHT

Chet's room window.

> CHET (O.S.)
> Are you crazy!?

INT. CHET'S ROOM

Chet looks uninspired by the proposition.

> MAX
> Will you help?

> CHET
> Yeah sure, whatever you want.

> MAX
> Great! We'll start tomorrow.

> DOUG
> This is gonna be cool.

Chet gives a fake smile and does the "thumbs up".

> CHET
> Cool.

Doug and Max leave in excitement. Chet stops smiling.

                    CHET (CONT'D)
          This is gonna suck.

BEGIN MONTAGE -- PREPARATION

--Chet, Max and Doug check out clothes at the store.

--THE TECH CREW prepare for the party, building the stage.

--In his room, Max draws plans on his notebook. The numbers
fly around his head. This time they connect perfectly.

--Chet tries on a variety of jeans and shirts on Max.

--Max shows his plans to Doug around Doug's living room
table. They argue over details. (MOS)

--Doug distracts the party crew at the community site. In the
background, Max tampers with the stage equipment.

--In the woods, Max and Doug test out a makeshift metal
device. Doug carefully turns it on. Sparks fly out.

--Doug talks to Amanda at the lake. He shows her a flyer of
the party. Amanda doesn't look interested, Doug tries to
convince her. (MOS)

--Max walks out of the dressing room wearing a very cool-
looking ensemble. Chet genuinely gives the "thumbs up".

--Chet, Max and Doug walk through the forest with a bunch of
bags full of clothes. The sun is about to set.

- END MONTAGE

EXT. SCHRODINGER HOUSE - NIGHT

The Schrodinger family car waits in front of the house. Chet
is in the driver's seat. Doug and Rose stand outside.

                    DOUG
          Come on! The party started already!

                    MAX (O.S.)
          I'll be right down!

Rose tries to straighten Doug's hair.

                    DOUG
          Mom!

                    ROSE
          Just one more touch.

Rose straightens a final piece on Doug's hair.

                    ROSE (CONT'D)
          Come home no later that ten. Don't
          drink too much soda.

                    DOUG
          I know.

                    ROSE
          I don't want you to mess around
          with older kids.

                    DOUG
          I know.

                    ROSE
          And don't…

Doug pulls himself back.

                    DOUG
          Mom, I know! Don't worry about me.
          I'll be fine.

Rose smiles and kisses Doug on the forehead.

                    ROSE
          I know.

INT. MAX'S ROOM - NIGHT

Max straightens his clothes, checking himself out in front of
the mirror.

There's a knock on the door. Evelyn sneaks her head in--

                    EVELYN
          May I come in?

                    MAX
          Sure.

Evelyn walks in and smiles in a warm way.

                    EVELYN
          You look very handsome.

                    MAX
          Thanks.

Evelyn straightens out Max's shirt.

> EVELYN
> Amanda will be thrilled to see you.

Max turns around.

> MAX
> How do you know about Amanda?

> EVELYN
> Believe me, mothers know. We have a
> sixth sense when it comes to our
> children. Also, Doug told Rose and
> Rose told me.

> MAX
> So, your sixth sense. What does it
> tell you now?

> EVELYN
> It tells me that everything will be
> just fine.

Max smiles. Evelyn kisses Max on the forehead.

> EVELYN (CONT'D)
> I'll be downstairs. And hurry up. I
> have a surprise.

> MAX
> What is it?

> EVELYN
> You'll see.

Evelyn leaves. Max looks around the room and notices H.G. He approaches his cage.

> MAX
> Goodbye, old friend. I have to
> leave you for a while.

INT. LIVING ROOM - NIGHT

Max walks downstairs. Evelyn stands at the entrance.

> MAX
> So, what's the surprise?

Evelyn points at the door. Sandy enters. He looks pale.

Sandy and Max smile at each other. They look like they want to talk in private.

                    EVELYN
          I'll go see if Chet's ready.

Evelyn leaves. Sandy groans in pain as he sits.

                    MAX
          Are you okay? You don't look good.

                    SANDY
          Don't worry about me.

Sandy gives out a slight cough.

                    SANDY (CONT'D)
          So, you're really gonna do this?

Max leans on the wall, unsure of himself.

                    MAX
          I'm not sure if I'll be able to
          pull it off.

Sandy tries to stand up.

                    SANDY
          I knew you'd say that.

Sandy manages to stand up. He pulls out a folded piece of
paper from his pocket.

Sandy gives the paper to Max. Max looks confused.

                    SANDY (CONT'D)
          Don't look until you get there. It
          will help you just in case you
          feel, anxious.

Max puts the paper in his pocket. He looks back at Sandy.

                    MAX
          Who are you?

Sandy pats Max on the shoulder.

                    SANDY
          Go on. She's waiting.

Max hugs Sandy and leaves. Evelyn approaches Sandy.

                    EVELYN
          Are you feeling alright?

>   SANDY
>   I'm fine. I'm sorry, I forgot to
>   thank you for this.

Evelyn nods. There's an awkward silence.

>   SANDY (CONT'D)
>   Listen, Evelyn, I know you have a
>   lot of questions about me but…

>   EVELYN
>   Don't worry about it. I'm just
>   happy he finally made some friends.
>   Even if they are a middle-aged man
>   and probably the weirdest kid I
>   have ever seen.

Sandy laughs. Evelyn joins him. Evelyn hugs Sandy.

>   EVELYN (CONT'D)
>   Thank you for being here.

Tears run down Sandy and Evelyn's faces. The hug feels right
to both of them.

Evelyn lets go of Sandy. She looks enchanted.

>   EVELYN (CONT'D)
>   I don't think I ever told you but,
>   you have beautiful eyes.

Sandy shyly laughs.

>   SANDY
>   Thank you. I got them from someone
>   very special.

EXT. STREET

Evelyn exits the house. He kisses Max.

>   ROSE
>   Bye sweetie. Have fun.

>   DOUG
>   Bye mom.

Doug hops in the front seat. The car leaves.

Rose looks after the car, teary-eyed.

>   ROSE
>   They grow up so fast.

She wipes her eyes.

INT. SCHRODINGER FAMILY CAR (MOVING) - NIGHT

Max sits in the middle of the back seat, worried.

He pulls out the note and looks at it. Sandy's voice resounds
in his head as he reads--

> SANDY (V.O.)
> An old woman chokes on her dinner.
> A tall man drops his book to help
> her. The doctor yells "Make room.
> Let her breathe." Answer the phone.

Max looks confused.

EXT. COMMUNITY GATHERING SITE / ENTRANCE — NIGHT

The family car pulls over at the side of the road. Max and
Doug get out.

Max turns to Chet, who remains in the driver's seat.

> MAX
> You sure you don't wanna join us?

> CHET
> Hang around with a bunch of fifteen-
> year-olds? I don't think so.

Max laughs.

> CHET (CONT'D)
> You have fun buddy. Show them what
> you're made of.

Chet offers his knuckle. Max taps it with his.

EXT. COMMUNITY GATHERING SITE — NIGHT

There's a considerable crowd of young people gathered around
the stage.

A bonfire burns in the middle of the crowd. The band plays a
contemporary song.

Doug and Amanda listen to the band at the front.

Doug dances like a monkey while Amanda looks misplaced.

> AMANDA
> Why did you drag me here? I feel
> weird around large groups.

                         DOUG
               Don't worry. It'll be worth it.

                         AMANDA
               How?

                         DOUG
               You'll see.

Doug looks at his watch.

                         DOUG (CONT'D)
               Oops. I gotta go. Just chill here.

Doug runs off.

                         AMANDA
               But, wha...?

EXT. BACKSTAGE - NIGHT

Max sneaks in back stage. He waits alone. He looks unsure of
himself. He peeks at the crowd.

He looks at Amanda. She looks bored.

                         MAX
               I can't do this.

Max turns around and tries to leave through the audience.
It's too crowded. He notices--

The common area shack next to the stage. The back door leads
to the other side of the forest.

Max runs to the shack.

Right after Max runs off, Doug appears, whispering.

                         DOUG
               Max? I'm ready.

Doug looks around.

                         DOUG (CONT'D)
               Max!?

INT. COMMON AREA SHACK - NIGHT

Max walks around the tables of people talking, eating and
playing card games. He heads for the exit.

                         OLD MAN (O.S.)
               Somebody help her! She's choking!!

Max immediately stops. He turns to look--

An OLD WOMAN chokes on her food. A TALL MAN drops his book and runs to help the woman.

Everyone stops what they are doing to focus on the woman.

The tall man jumps on the old woman and administers the Heimlich maneuver.

The old woman spits out her food and takes in all the air she humanly can.

A MAN approaches the crowd.

> DOCTOR
> I'm a doctor. Stand back. Make
> room, let her breathe.

The phone next to Max rings. Intimidated yet curious, Max picks up the phone.

> MAX
> Hello?

> SANDY (ON PHONE)
> You can't do this.

> MAX
> Sandy?

INT. SANDY'S ROOM

Sandy sits in the middle of an empty room. He looks sick.

> SANDY
> You can't do this Max. You can't
> run away.

INTERCUT — SANDY'S ROOM / COMMON AREA SHACK

> MAX
> How did you...?

> SANDY
> What if I told you that I know for
> a fact this is your last chance to
> tell Amanda what you feel about
> her? Are you really going to let
> her slip through your fingers just
> because you are scared?

                    MAX
          I don't know Sandy. It's just not
          me. I just can't...

                    SANDY
          It's not you? Do you really believe
          that? You are what you make of
          yourself kid. You can either run
          away now and keep running, or you
          can face your fears and prove
          yourself wrong. Which one is it
          going to be Max? Which one?

EXT. BACKSTAGE - NIGHT

                    DOUG
          Max? Max?

Doug walks back in disappointment.

                    MAX (O.S.)
          Doug.

Doug turns around in relief.

                    DOUG
          Where were you?

                    MAX
          I was running.

                    DOUG
          Are you ready?

                    MAX
          No, but let's do it.

Max and Doug laugh. Doug pulls his laptop out of his backpack
and hooks it up to the projection system.

                    DOUG
          Let's hope this works.

COMMUNITY GATHERING SITE

The band keeps playing their song. All of a sudden, the power
is cut off. The area is drenched in moonlit darkness.

The band members look at each other, confused. The crowd
boos. "BRING IT ON HOME TO ME" by THE ANIMALS blare out of
the speakers.

Smoke comes out beneath the stage. The band members cough.
Soon, they walk off the stage, leaving it empty.

The smoke fills the stage. Air is blown into specific parts
of the smoke. The smoke spells, "I LOVE YOU"

Another puff of air beneath that spells, "AMANDA"

Amanda watches front and center, dumbfounded.

Through the smoke, a figure walks closer to the center.

The smoke clears. It's Max. In between the confused murmurs
of the crowd, he stands fearless.

He looks for Amanda. He finds her in the middle of the crowd.
She has tears in her eyes, smiling from ear to ear.

Max slowly descends the stage. Amidst the smoke, he gently
kisses her.

She kisses him back. Everyone applauds and woos.

Doug watches with pride. He joins in the applause.

                    DOUG
          Woo!! Way to go buddy!!

Amanda looks at her watch.

                    MAX
          Let me guess. You have to go home.

Amanda laughs.

                    AMANDA
          Not for a couple of hours.

Max is relieved.

                    AMANDA (CONT'D)
          But I do have to go to... You know.

                    MAX
          What? Oh sure.

Amanda shyly smiles.

                    AMANDA
          I'll be right back.

Amanda walks away. She turns around and waves at Max. Max
waves back.

As soon as Amanda is out of sight, Max jumps on Doug.

                    MAX
          Did you see that!!?

                    DOUG
          Calm down man. You're acting weird.

                    MAX
          I couldn't have done this without
          you. You're my best friend.

Doug has a reassuring smile, as if he completed his mission.

                    DOUG
          Thanks.

                    MAX
          I can't wait to tell Sandy.

INT. SANDY'S LIVING ROOM — NIGHT

There's a knock on the door.

                    MAX (O.S.)
          Sandy? Are you home?

The door opens. Max, Doug and Amanda walk in.

                    MAX (CONT'D)
          Sandy?

They all look around the room. It is a mess.

Max walks upstairs.

                    MAX (CONT'D)
          Sandy where are you?

SANDY'S ROOM

Max walks in.

                    MAX
          Sandy, are you alright?

Max looks at the floor.

                    MAX (CONT'D)
          Oh no!

Sandy lays on the ground, unconscious. Albert desperately
licks his face, trying to resuscitate him.

Max holds Sandy. He starts crying.

                    MAX (CONT'D)
          Sandy, what happened? What
          happened!?

EXT. STREETS — NIGHT

An ambulance through the streets, sirens blaring.

INT. HOSPITAL CORRIDOR - DAWN

The corridor is full of worried visitors. Evelyn, Chet, Doug
and Max are among them.

They all look sleepless. Max's very worried.

DR. SONI, 40, exits the room. He looks baffled. Evelyn and
Max jump up in anticipation.

                    EVELYN
          Doctor, how is he?

Dr. Soni tries to hold his thoughts together.

                    DR. SONI
          We have been able to resuscitate
          him for now but I... I don't know
          how to tell you this.

                    EVELYN
          What is it?

                    DR. SONI
          He's dying.

Everyone looks shocked. Max starts crying.

                    EVELYN
          What's wrong with him?

                    DR. SONI
          We have no idea. I've never seen
          anything like this.

                    EVELYN
          Isn't there something you can do?

Dr. Soni averts his eyes.

                    DR. SONI
          I'm sorry.

A NURSE comes out of the room.

                        NURSE
          Max Schrodinger?

                        MAX
          Yes?

                        NURSE
          He wants to talk to you. Alone.

Max looks at Evelyn with tears in his eyes.

                        EVELYN
          Go ahead sweetie. We'll be here.

INT. PATIENT ROOM - DAWN

Sandy is hooked on to various life-support devices. He's in a
half stood-up position on the bed.

Max walks in. He looks destroyed.

                        SANDY
             Take a seat.

Max sits on the chair next to the bed. He tries to hold back
his tears.

                        MAX
          What happened to you?

                        SANDY
          It's time I tell you. Did you bring
          my stuff?

                        MAX
          Whatever we could find.

Max points to a table full of stuff. In the middle stands The
red file Max saw earlier at Sandy's house.

                        SANDY
          Bring me that file.

Max picks up the file. It's filled with documents.

                        SANDY (CONT'D)
          In there, you will find the
          blueprints of a machine I
          supervised as part of a classified
          project. Building it was my dream.
          I worked on it all my life.

Max looks like he recognizes the files as he flips through.

                    SANDY (CONT'D)
          We tested it on animals. The
          results were as perfect as they
          could be. But when it was time to
          try it on human subjects, it was a
          disaster. We found out it affected
          the human cell structure in
          unmanageable ways.

In between the files, there are pictures of a YOUNG MAN. He
looks sick. He looks sicker with every picture.

                    MAX
          What was the machine?

                    SANDY
          It took my assistant two months to
          die. Immediately after his death,
          the project was trashed and I was
          fired. I didn't have anything left
          to live for anymore. So I broke in
          and used the machine on myself to
          do what I had always planned.

Max looks at the final page of the file. He looks shocked.

                    MAX
          Sandy, what was the machine!?

                    SANDY
          Max, I want you to know...

                    MAX
          What was the machine!!?

Sandy looks at Max straight in the eyes.

                    SANDY
          I think you know what it is.

Max drops the file in shock.

The file SLAMS OPEN on the floor, exposing the documents--

ON TOP OF THE DOCUMENTS IS THE BLUEPRINT OF THE OCTAGON-
SHAPED MACHINE MAX HAS BEEN WORKING ON SINCE THE BEGINNING.

Max looks at an ID CARD on the floor. He picks up the card
and looks at it. It's an I.S.R.O. security card with Sandy's
face on it.

THE CARD READS: "Max Schrodinger"

"BIRTH DATE: 12/22/2000"

"ISSUE DATE: May 2053"

                    MAX
          This can't be true. It just can't
          be true.

                    SANDY
          It is true.

                    MAX
          You mean, you… I… we made it?

Sandy smiles and nods.

                    SANDY
          We did.

                    MAX
          But… But what the hell are you
          doing here? I…

                    SANDY
          You wanted to use the machine to
          convince dad to come back.

Max thinks.

                    MAX
          You were there.

**INT. OLD SCHRODINGER APARTMENT / MAX'S ROOM — NIGHT
(FLASHBACK)**

Young Max looks outside the window.

EXT. STREET

The man wearing a hooded brown coat standing next to Philip's
car lifts up his head--

It's Sandy. He looks intently at the car driving away with
Max's father in it.

> SANDY (V.O.)
> I tried everything with him.

INT. HOSPITAL / PATIENT ROOM — DAWN (PRESENT)

> SANDY
> But he wouldn't change his mind for
> anyone, including his own son.

Sandy looks outside at the beautiful view of the hills.

> SANDY (CONT'D)
> So I decided to change the way I
> lived my life. I used the machine
> one last time before destroying it.
> I came here, the only vacation I
> ever had. The only chance I could
> have to turn you into the person I
> wanted to be.

Max cries. Sandy looks back at Max.

> SANDY (CONT'D)
> I could act on every new memory
> that was created by my presence.
> That's how I knew what was going to
> happen before they happened. With
> my interference, I was able to get
> a brand new past, with incredible,
> brand new memories.

Sandy looks deep into Max's eyes.

> SANDY (CONT'D)
> Do me a favor.

> MAX
> Anything.

> SANDY
> Tell our mom I always loved her.
> You have no idea how hard it was to
> keep myself from holding her and
> never letting go.

> MAX
> I will.

Sandy approaches Max. He whispers.

> SANDY
> I want you to know you will lead a
> wonderful life Max. I want you to
> appreciate every second of it.

Sandy leans back on his pillow, smiling with complete bliss.

> SANDY (CONT'D)
> I can see it now. It's so,
> beautiful.

--BEGIN MONTAGE

--Max's future flashes before Sandy's eyes.

--Max, 15, kisses Amanda, 15, on top of a hill at sundown.

--Max, 18, smiles for his graduation photo with Doug, 18, and Amanda, 18. Evelyn takes the picture.

--Max and Amanda's wedding. Max slides the ring on Amanda's finger. They kiss.

--Amanda screams in pain as she gives birth on a hospital bed. Max holds Amanda's hands while hyperventilating.

--Max, 35, plays basketball with his SON, 5, on his backyard. They both miss all the shots.

--Max, 40, hangs out with his friends at a bar. Doug, 40, stands next to him, holds up his drink.

> DOUG (40)
> I want to propose a toast to my
> best friend...

--Max, 50, now looks like Sandy, rests on a recliner in the backyard. He watches his wife and TWO KIDS play. He has a smile on his face.

> MATCH CUT TO:

INT. HOSPITAL / PATIENT ROOM - DAWN

Sandy lies unconscious on his bed, with a smile on his face.

The nurse covers his face with a blanket.

INT. HOSPITAL CORRIDOR - DAWN

Max exits the patient's room with tears in his eyes.

Amanda gets up and approaches Max.

> MAX
> He's gone.

Max weeps. Amanda hugs him.

Slowly, Evelyn, Chet and Doug join Amanda with the hug. They remain attached as one.

> MAX (35) (V.O.) (CONT'D)
> I never told anyone what happened
> in that room.

EXT. SCHRODINGER HOUSE / PORCH – DAWN

Evelyn and Max exit the house. Evelyn closes the door.

> EVELYN
> Are you ready?

Max nods.

EXT. FOREST - DAWN

Empty, beautiful. The road shines under the dawning sun. Evelyn and Max walk down the forest.

> MAX (35) (V.O.)
> To this day, my mother still has no
> idea why I dragged her outside at
> five in the morning. But I knew
> Sandy would have wanted me to do
> this, with someone very special.

Max looks behind him. Albert runs to catch up with Max.

Albert runs through the forest with all his might, as if he's a puppy all over again. Max runs along with him.

EXT. LAKE - DAWN

Albert runs into the lake and soaks in the cool water. Max follows him.

The boy and the dog play in the water like there is no tomorrow, soaking in life as it unrolls with every step.

Evelyn watches them with joy.

> MAX (35) (V.O.)
> Two months later, Albert died of
> old age. We buried him next to
> Sandy.

TITLE CARD: "TWENTY YEARS LATER"

EXT. CHAMPAIGN SHOPPING AREA – DAY

It's early in the morning. The mall is moderately crowded. A car parks next to the stores.

                    MAX (35) (V.O.)
          I do have a happy life, as Sandy
          predicted. I'm still very close to
          my family. Amanda and I have been
          married for ten years. We have two
          beautiful kids. Of course one of
          them is named Sandy.

MAX (35), walks out of the car and heads for the shops.

                    MAX (35) (V.O.)
          I'm still a successful scientist.
          Maybe I'm not as great at
          everything as much as I hoped I'd
          be. But then again, who is?

He looks intently at the stores, looking for the right one.

                    MAX (35) (V.O.)
          I still try to honor Sandy and live
          everyday fuller than the last. He
          believed in his memories so much
          that he was willing to sacrifice
          his life for them. And in many
          ways, he succeeded.

Max (35) stops in front of one of the stores. He smiles.

                    MAX (35) (V.O.)
          But although I managed to build an
          entirely new life for myself…

Turns out he is standing in front of a pet store.

                    MAX (35) (V.O.)
          …some things never change.

Old Max approaches the store and looks inside.

A PUPPY stands alone, looking confused in his glass cage.
Max and the puppy look at each other.

                    MAX (35)
          Hello Albert.

Max walks in the store.

                    THE END

ABOUT THE SCREENWRITER

Oktay Ege Kozak is a screenwriter, script coach and film critic. He works as a reader for some of the leading screenplay coverage companies in Hollywood, and is also a film critic for The Playlist, DVD Talk, and Beyazperde. He has a BA in Film Theory and an MFA in Screenwriting. He lives near Portland, OR, with his wife, daughter, and two King Charles Spaniels.

120pages

EXPOSURE. CREDIBILITY. PROFIT.

PUBLISH YOUR SCREENPLAY WITH **120pages**!

You've spent countless hours — maybe years — writing your screenplay. You believe it in it, but it has not yet been picked up for production.

By publishing your screenplay with 120pages, you will:

- Earn income from your work
- Give your screenplay exposure
- Build your credibility as a screenwriter

Visit **120pages.com** today to learn more!

www.ingramcontent.com/pod-product-compliance
Lightning Source LLC
Chambersburg PA
CBHW071815190726
48292CB00008B/2846